<u>Dedications</u>

I would like to dedicate this book to my mother **Diane Murphy**. My mother accepted me for who I was and has always been my biggest supporter, she accepts anybody for who they are and has one of the biggest hearts. I love you.

Another dedication is to my fiancé **Christian Prior**, he supports me with everything I do, and he will do anything to help me achieve my goals. I am so happy we found each other; I Love you so much.

Final dedication is to my best friend **Tony Stanley**, I could not ask for a better supportive friend. The friendship was destined to blossom from the age of fourteen to what we are now thirty seven. Here is to the rest of our lives together.

Cover Art by: Katherine Weil

Love Kills

The man lay in his bed, wrapped in peaceful slumber.
The room was designed with a standard colour
scheme of ivory walls and black and ivory furniture.
The bed, a solid double covered in cream linens and
with black pillows, dominated the space. On the
wooden bedside table sat a charging mobile phone, a
lamp casting a soft glow, and an unfinished glass of
water. Suddenly, Connor's alarm blared at 5:30am,
rudely disrupting his rest. He grumbled as he
reluctantly climbed out of bed, throwing back the
duvet. Slipping into his familiar black slippers, he
made his way towards the door of the bedroom.
Pulling on the handle, he revealed a narrow hallway
leading to a flight of stairs. Carefully descending
each step, Connor started his day with slow
determination.

Connor made his way down the stairs, glancing at
the photographs on the walls. A small smile formed
on his face as he descended each step. When he
reached the bottom of the staircase, he stepped into
the kitchen, with its modern mix of chrome and

wooden cabinets. The kettle, a subtle shade of grey, was sitting on the counter. As he waited for it to boil, Connor's mind wandered to his job and why he had to wake up early every day. Despite this, he loved his work and looked forward to each workday, especially when it was payday.

Connor finished the last few sips of his lukewarm tea and glanced at the clock - it was 6:10am. He had an hour before he needed to leave for work. Placing his mug on the table, he climbed back up the stairs and into the bathroom for a refreshing shower. The warm water felt soothing as it cascaded over his body, causing him to let out a content sigh. Once he was dry with a soft, fluffy towel, he entered his bedroom, which faced directly towards the bathroom. In one corner stood his wardrobe with black painted doors, like a silent guardian. Upon opening it, he was met with a chaotic mix of clothes that held different memories and emotions for Connor. After much thought, he settled on a pair of blue skinny chinos, a white Superman t-shirt from which it held sentimental value reminding him of his younger years when he used to watch Superman, and he picked out a red cardigan to combat the morning chill. With a quick dab of gel and some styling, his blonde hair fell perfectly into its signature spiky style.

At the age of thirty, Connor still took great pride in his thick, blonde hair. He meticulously styled it every morning to achieve a seemingly effortless look. He also made sure to brush his teeth and apply deodorant and aftershave before leaving his room. With a satisfied nod at his reflection, Connor left his bedroom and closed the door behind him. The hallway was dimly lit, but he could see well enough thanks to the light streaming in from the window at the end of the hall. He descended the stairs until he reached the bottom floor.

Connor stood in front of the door; a large, dark wooden structure that seemed to tower over him. He reached into his cabinet next to the door and retrieved both his house keys and car keys before twisting the doorknob and exiting the house. A few small steps led down to a narrow path, which wound through a beautiful garden maintained by Connor himself. The luscious grass appeared radiant in the morning light, and the hedges surrounding it added an element of seclusion.

Connor gave his home a final look before heading towards his car, a sleek blue Corsa. The sunlight dancing through the nearby trees bounced off its shiny exterior as he settled into the driver's seat and drove away to begin his day.

Connor drives to work while jamming out to his favourite playlist. Today, it's filled with upbeat tracks from Kesha's 'Animal' album, but he enjoys all types of music. People may judge him for having a Dannii Minogue coffee mug and a Britney Spears calendar, but Connor does not care about their opinions. It's already 6:35am. He likes to arrive early so he can prepare teas and coffees for the staff before they come in. Working in a care home has been the best job Connor has had since he turned eighteen.

It is now 7:00am, and it is time to go to the handover for the morning.

Connor takes a seat in the handover room and notices Susan entering. She has been his closest colleague for many years now, with her long blonde hair, slender figure, and glamorous fashion sense. Standing at five foot five, she exudes confidence but also has a kind heart hidden beneath her upfront demeanour. Despite her boldness, she can be quite shy deep down.

'Hey there, Connor. How's it going, buddy?' Susan asks.

'Not too bad, thanks. And you?' Connor responds.

'Doing well, thanks. It's a pretty early morning today, huh?' Susan remarks.

'Yeah, I've never been a fan of these early starts,' Connor agrees.

At precisely 7:05am, the handover meeting began. The staff briefed everyone on important information from the previous day. After the handover ended, it was time to be assigned our daily tasks. I would be helping residents with their personal hygiene and meals throughout the day, specifically those with Huntington's Disease, a degenerative brain condition that affects movement, thinking, and emotions. Our duties also included supporting them with eating and drinking due to their complex needs. Despite working a fourteen-hour shift, it was a great day filled with laughter and games with the residents. Connor and Susan consistently maintain a positive attitude and strive to improve the quality of life for those in their care. As 9:00pm rolled around, it was time to clock out and head home for the night. Both

Connor and Susan were ready to end their shift and eagerly logged out for the day.

'Hey Susan, are we still meeting up tomorrow evening for a drink?' Connor asks.

'Yes, just the three of us, right?' Susan confirms.

'Yeah, it will be me, you, and Rex,' Connor affirms.

'Awesome. I actually have a couple of friends who will be there too, is that alright?' Susan checks in.

'Of course! The more the merrier,' Connor replies.

'Great. See you tomorrow then,' Susan says with a smile.

'Yep, see you tomorrow,' Connor responds before walking away.

After driving home, Connor takes a refreshing shower and changes into his comfortable night clothes. He enjoys having some time alone, but sometimes he cannot help feeling a little lonely. It is almost 10:00pm, and Connor is cozily lounging on the couch in his onesie while catching up on some TV shows. He has the next day off from work and is excited about meeting up with his great friends

Susan and Rex for drinks in the evening. Before calling it a night, Connor updates his Facebook status to let everyone know about his plans. He finally goes to bed at 11:00pm and falls asleep almost instantly as soon as his head touches the pillow.

After waking up, Connor puts on the kettle to make himself a cup of tea. He takes some time to relax before tackling some housework. Despite being single for two years, Connor is content with his life, though he would not mind being in a relationship. The rest of his day is spent casually moving around his home, completing chores and cooking himself dinner. Later in the evening, he gets ready to meet up with friends for a drink.

As evening falls, Connor indulges in a long bath and shaves before heading out. He opts for a simple black t-shirt and a bold red tie, paired with sleek black trousers. Some have commented that his outfit resembles the style of the lead singer from Green Day.

At 7:00pm, Connor prepares himself to go out. He settles at the dining table in his kitchen and enjoys a small glass of whisky and coke before heading out. After finishing his drink, he exits his house and meets up with his friends to walk to their favourite gay pub in Southport.

They rendezvous just outside the pub, a quaint yellow cottage with ivy crawling up its walls, known as The Blue Dolphin. Connor, Rex and Susan all enter together and approach the bar.

Connor and Rex have been inseparable since they first met at the age of 12 in school. Their friendship quickly flourished as they did everything together and supported each other through every challenge. Rex, who was tall and slim with dark brown hair and dark brown eyes, was often praised for his good looks and even told he could be a model. At 16, Connor mustered up the courage to tell Rex his biggest secret: he was gay. To his surprise, Rex revealed that he too was gay. The two best friends were stunned to find out they shared the same truth and from that day on, their friendship only grew stronger. They no longer had to hide or worry about what the other might think, and their bond became unbreakable. Coming out to each other only brought them closer together and changed their lives for the better.

In a busy gay bar in Southport, Connor treats his friends to drinks. The pub is a welcoming space for people of all orientations, and fights are a rare occurrence in its friendly atmosphere.

'I'll be right back, just got to use the restroom,' Connor announces to his friends.

'Hurry up, we're about to go smoke a cigarette,' Rex urges.

'Got it, no problem,' Connor agrees.

Connor rises from his seat and heads towards the bathroom, glancing back to see if his friends will follow for a smoke break or wait for him. But as he turns around, something stops him in his tracks.

Connor stumbles backwards, exclaiming, 'Oops, I'm so sorry!' His voice is filled with regret as he realizes he just bumped into someone. The person he collided with was about average height, with piercing dark eyes and spikey hair. They were dressed in a professional grey suit with a black tie.

'Sorry about that mate, I wasn't paying attention.' The stranger reassures Connor.

'No, it's my fault. I am quite clumsy and tend to walk around with my eyes closed most of the time.' Connor replies sheepishly.

The stranger laughs and says, 'same here. Don't worry about it, let's just forget it happened.'

Feeling guilty, Connor offers to buy the stranger another drink since most of his was now on the floor. But the stranger surprises him by saying, 'No way,

let me get you a drink for feeling bad about being so clumsy.'

Connor laughs and agrees, but not before asking for the stranger's name. 'Oh, it's Clyde. And yours?' Clyde responds with a smirk.

Connor introduces himself and Clyde comments, 'I like that name.'

Pleased with each other's company, they decide to grab another round of drinks. 'What can I get you?' Clyde asks.

Surprised at Clyde's generosity, Connor asks if he wants him to buy him a drink as well. Clyde smiles and says, 'You're quite the character, aren't you? No, honestly it is fine. I want to buy you a drink.'

Clyde buys Connor a drink and then they chat some more at the bar and ten minutes pass and Connor realises he is supposed to be outside with his friends having a cigarette,

'Clyde, I meant to be outside with my friends. Do you want to come out with me so I can have a cigarette?'

Clyde says, 'oh you smoke. That is a bad habit, yeah that is cool. I will come out with you.'

Connor says, 'I know it is a nasty habit and way too expensive. I do need to stop. I do not smoke that often, but I do smoke more when I drink, to be honest.'

Connor and Clyde make their way outside to the smoking area, where Connor then sees his mates.

'Hey guys,' Connor says.

'Where have you bloody been?' Rex blurts out.

'Oh, I bashed into someone, knocked his drink on the floor and he bought me a drink. I know I didn't get it either.' Connor says.

Connor introduces Clyde to his mates.

'Hey everyone, this is Clyde. We just met at the bar, and he kindly bought me a drink. Clyde, these are my friends Rex and Susan. Guys, meet Clyde.'

Susan interjects, 'Yeah, we get it Connor. He bought you a drink. No need to make a big deal out of it.'

Connor responds, 'Thanks for pointing that out, Susan, right in front of him.'

Clyde chimes in, 'Don't worry Connor. It's actually my first time buying someone a drink.'

Susan adds, 'Looks like you two have something in common then.'

Connor sighs, 'Thanks for not being subtle about it Susan.'

Clyde invites, 'Come on, let's sit down and chat. Tell me a little more about yourself, Connor.'

They both take a seat and Connor begins to share.

'I'm thirty years old and have been single for the past two years. My ex was great, but things just didn't work out in the end. I currently live alone which has its pros and cons.'

Clyde responds, 'That's cool. I actually live alone too and I am thirty two years old. It has been about seven years since my last relationship.'

Shocked, Connor exclaims, 'Wow, you've been single for seven years? That must be tough.'

Clyde responded, 'I have been on the road for seven long years, but my ex didn't want to join me. He could not understand my desire to explore the world.'

Connor nods in agreement and says, 'I feel the same way. I want to find someone to settle down with and build a future together.'

Clyde responds, 'It can be tough out there with so many people just looking for casual hookups. That is not my style.'

Connor asks, 'What do you do for work?'

Clyde replies, 'I have my own business creating and selling computer software to companies.'

Connor then asks, 'And what about you? What kind of work do you do?'

'Wow, that's great,' Connor responds. 'I work at a care home, so it's not a high-paying job, but it covers my living expenses.'

Clyde interjects, 'Don't worry about hiding your salary. It is okay. Money is not the most important thing, and you are making a difference in people's lives. That is more fulfilling than my job. Well done.'

Connor smiles and says, 'Thank you for saying that. It means a lot.'

Connor and Clyde continue their conversation, even after all of Connor's friends have gone home. It's just the two of them left now. They both decide to take a stroll, enjoying each other's company and thinking about how nice the other person is. Eventually, Clyde suggests walking Connor home, and Connor happily agrees as they begin their journey. Along the way, Clyde asks Connor a question.

'Would it be alright if I had your number so I could take you out on a proper date?' asks Clyde.

Connor eagerly responds, 'I would love that! Thank you for asking.'

As they arrive at Connor's house, he hands Clyde his number.

'Here you go. You can contact me anytime, through text or phone call,' says Connor.

'Thank you, I will do that right away. You should go inside and get out of the cold,' suggests Clyde.

With a smirk, Connor replies, 'Yes, I will do just that.'

Clyde bids him a good night, to which Connor responds in kind before heading inside. They both look forward to talking again soon.

After Clyde leaves, Connor enters his home and makes his way to the front room, smiling as he thinks about the evening. While getting ready for bed, a familiar feeling of excitement rushes through his body, one that he has not felt in years. It is a feeling he had almost forgotten about, but now it fills him with pure joy. Suddenly, his phone buzzes and he has a text from Clyde coming through.

(Clyde) it was great meeting you tonight, Connor, can we have a date tomorrow after you finish work? I was thinking maybe just grabbing a bite to eat and go from there? xx

(Connor) yes, it was good meeting you tonight. I loved our chat and yeah that would be great because I am always starving after the shift :) xx

(Clyde) lovely ok then, so can I pick you up at 9:30pm from your house? Is that ok? xx

(Connor) yeah that will be fine, and I can get ready at work beforehand, well good night, Clyde. See you tomorrow :-) xx

(Clyde) that is good, yes goodnight, Connor and have a good shift tomorrow and I will see you at 9:30pm sharp. xx

Connor falls to sleep and is so happy and overjoyed he has finally got a date with someone that he falls to sleep so fast.

13th February

At 5:30am sharp, Connor is awoken by his alarm. He quickly gets ready for work and heads out, choosing to blast out love songs instead of his usual playlist during the drive. When he arrives at his place of work, he joins in on the morning handover meeting and jumps right into his tasks for the day. Despite being busy and productive, Connor cannot shake off the fluttery feeling in his stomach. As the day goes on, time seems to pass by quickly. But just as he reaches the halfway mark of his shift, Susan approaches him with something to discuss.

'The guy you were chatting with last night was quite handsome. Did you manage to get his number?'

With a grin on Connor's face, he adds, 'I did more than that, Susan.'

Susan responds with shock, 'Oh my gosh, you sneaky minx, you've never done that before? Are you serious?'

Connor says, 'oh my god shut up. No, I gave him my number, and he is taking me for something to eat after the shift. He is picking me up from my house.'

Susan says 'really? no sexual favours or kissy kissy?'

Connor replies, NO, and no one says that…. Ever.

Susan congratulates Connor, saying 'good job for not engaging in any sexual activities. The last thing you want is to give in on the first meeting. He would probably tell others that you're awful in bed.'

Connor retorts, 'You have no idea how I am in the bedroom. For all you know, I could be a complete stud.'

Susan shakes her head and responds, 'No, I've already read the clues in the graffiti on the bathroom walls at the gay bar.'

'You're joking, right? First off, I used the boys' bathroom, and you use the girls', and secondly, what kind of gay guy would write 'Connor Summers is a lousy lay' in a girl's bathroom?' Connor retorts with a sarcastic tone.

Susan says, ' oh yeah, never mind. Well, I hope it's a good night tonight then and remember if you want to play, remember to be safe.'

Connor says, 'oh god get out of here, you sicko.'

As their shift comes to an end, Connor and Susan leave the care home and start their drive home. Connor had already spent time at work preparing for the evening ahead, and as he drives home, he can't help but hope for a smooth and successful night. Finally arriving home at 9:15pm, all he has to do is brush his teeth and add a bit more aftershave before Clyde picks him up to take him out for the evening.

At 9:30pm, there is a knock on the door, and Connor goes to open the door.

'Clyde, hey, how are you?' Connor asks.

'I am really good, thank you. And how are you?' Clyde replied.

'I am good cheers. Are you ready? Do you want me to drive, or do you want to drive?' Connor asks.

No, it's ok. I would much prefer to drive. Clyde replied.

Clyde adds. 'Right, are you ready then? let's go. I thought we could go to the Mexican restaurant if that is ok with you?'

'Yeah, that sounds good to me,' Connor replies.

Connor and Clyde make their way across the street to where Clyde's shiny silver BMW is parked. They hop into the car and set off on their drive. As they cruise along, classical music fills the car, much to Connor's disappointment. However, he keeps his thoughts to himself as he knows Clyde has been a great host so far and he cannot complain about a little bit of classical music.

'So, what music do you like to listen to then, Connor?' Clyde asks.

'Well, I like anything really, but I've never really been a fan of classical music, but this is cool as it is kind of relaxing. I like the top 40 chart sort of music. My music type is weird I can like very poppy music to heavy metal.' Connor replied.

'That is lovely. Having a wide range variety of music, I am not really into anything poppy or charts, just my classical would do me,' Clyde says.

'Oh right, that is ok. Everyone is different, are they not? we all have different taste in music.' Connor says.

'Yeah, I am sure I could be persuaded to go to a pop concert if someone was to return the favour and come to the opera house with me,' Clyde hints.

'Yeah, I'm sure if that did happened, then the other person would 100% return the favour. Can you drink there?' Connor asks.

'Where? at the opera house?' Clyde asks.

'Yeah' Connor says.

'Yeah, of course you can,' Clyde answers.

'Oh, that's good then, just as long as I know you can drink loads there. I think I could deal with it a bit better; you know.' Connor says.

'Ok then,' Clyde says with a smile on his face. 'Well, we are here. Just got to park up then we can go in. Clyde says.

'Oh great, I get so hungry after working all day.' Connor says.

As they approached the Mexican restaurant, Connor and Clyde could not help but notice the brick exterior and neatly lined trees out front. The glass door beckoned them inside. However, as they walked towards it, Connor had a sudden realization - he could not handle spicy food. He mentally kicked himself for agreeing to this choice, purely because it was Clyde's first suggestion. 'This is going to be interesting,' he thought, but he decided to at least take a look at the menu before making any decisions.

Clyde opens the door for Connor. 'Aw thanks' Connor says.

'Hello gentlemen, can I help you tonight?' asks the server man.

The waiter donned a professional attire consisting of black trousers, a crisp white button-down shirt, and a bold red waistcoat layered over the shirt.

'Yes, I got a table booked for 9:45pm in the name of hunter,' Clyde replies.

'Welcome! Please follow me this way. Here is your designated table, and here are the menus. Would you like a drink while you peruse our options for your meal?' The server offered Connor and Clyde with a friendly smile.

'Yes, please. I will have a coca cola and Connor???' asks Clyde.

'I'll have the same cheers,' Connor replies.

The server quickly responds, 'Absolutely, I will bring that over to you right away.'

'So that's your surname then, hunter? oh I like that, Clyde hunter.' Connor says with a slight smile on his face.

'Yeah, hunter is my name, so what is yours?' Clyde asks.

'Its Summers' Connor answers.

'Oh, that is a really nice name, Connor summers.' Clyde says.

'Thank you, Clyde,' Connor replies.

'Here are your drinks, gentlemen,' the server man says.

'Thank you,' Clyde replies.

'Can I take your order?' the server man asks.

'Yeah, I will have a chili con carne please,' Clyde replies.

Oh well, I am not too sure. Maybe I will have the same thank you.' Connor says. 'it is not too hot, is it?' Connor adds.

'No, it is a very mild dish,' the server man answers.

'Oh good,' Connor says.

It should not take too long. We are not very busy right now, so we should be able to serve you in about fifteen minutes,' the server man informs Connor and Clyde.

'Ok then, thank you very much,' Clyde says.

'So, Connor summers. How has your day been?' Clyde asks.

'It's been good, thanks. It's a long old day, but we have good staff and good residents, so the days go pretty quick. How about yours?' Connor replied.

'It has been lovely, thank you. I did some more work for a new software that I am creating and got a company interested in buying it from me,' Clyde answers.

'Oh, wow amazing. That's so cool. I bet you get a lot of money for creating software.' Connor says.

'Yeah, it's a good little earner,' Clyde replies.

'Oh, that's good then. I wished I could earn lots of money,' Connor says.

'Oh, don't you worry about money, Connor,' Clyde replies.

As the waiter serves their food, Connor and Clyde continue to chat and get to know each other. This is one of the most thrilling aspects of meeting someone new, exchanging stories and learning about each other's interests. The time passes quickly as they enjoy each other's company. Once they finish their meals, they ask for the bill.

So how are we going to do this? Shall we pay half and half? Connor asks.

'No way, I am paying for it all. I really enjoyed tonight so much,' Clyde answers.

'No, you got to let me pay for some of it.' Connor asks.

'Nope, put your money away. I want to do this please,' Clyde says.

'Thank you then Clyde.' Connor says.

'Shall we go then?' Clyde asks.

'Yeah, let's get going. I am getting tired now where it's been a long old day,' Connor replies.

'Ok, come on then and I will get you home,' Clyde offers.

They both climb into the car and head off. After arriving at Connor's house, Clyde pulls over and shuts off the engine.

'I really honestly enjoyed tonight, Connor.' Clyde says.

'Yeah, me too. It was nice just chatting to you for a couple of hours without drink inside us,' Connor replies.

'Yeah, so are we going to do this again, yes?' Clyde asks.

'Yeah, sure, I would really love to do this again,' Connor replies.

'Is it ok if I give you a kiss goodnight?' Clyde asks.

'Oh, well. Yeah, sure I don't mind if you go in for a kiss,' Connor answers.

Clyde leans closer to Connor, and they both move in for a kiss. Their lips meet and linger for around five seconds, but it feels like a full minute to them.

'Wow, that was nice,' Connor says.

'Yeah, it was,' Clyde replies.

'Well, ok then, I shall see you soon,' Connor says.

'Yeah, sure, I will text you once I get in my home.' Clyde replied.

'Ok then Clyde and thank you again for tonight. It was really nice just chatting to you, speak to you soon. Bye.' Connor says.

'Yes, I have really enjoyed your company tonight. See you soon, bye,' Clyde answers.

Connor walks towards his door but turns back to check on Clyde's car. Clyde is still waiting, making sure that Connor gets inside safely. Connor unlocks his door with his key and glances back at Clyde before entering his house. Clyde waves goodbye and drives off. As soon as Connor is alone in his house, he feels a flutter of excitement in the pit of his stomach. 'That was incredible,' Connor thinks to himself. While waiting for a message from Clyde confirming he arrived home. Connor makes a cup of tea and smokes a cigarette. Ten minutes later, his phone starts ringing.

(Clyde) hi Connor, I am home now xx

(Connor) that is cool. What are you doing now? Are you going to bed? xx

(Clyde) yes, I will be in a minute. Are you free tomorrow? xx

(Connor) I am going to bed soon too, yeah, it is my day off tomorrow xx

(Clyde) that is great. I was wondering if you wanted to go out on an all-day date tomorrow unless you have already got plans? xx

(Connor) no I have got nothing planned so that would be great :-) xx

(Clyde) ok then, how about I will pick you up at 10am in the morning and we can go from there? xx

(Connor) yeah that is great. I will be ready by 10 then. I am excited :-) xx

(Clyde) that is great, yes, I am excited too ;-) night xx

(Connor) nighty night xx

14th February

The shrill sound of Connor's alarm pierces the quiet morning at 8:30am. He quickly jumps out of bed and heads to the kitchen to start the day with a cup of tea. As he sips his beverage, he takes a moment to contemplate what he and Clyde could do that day for fun. Suddenly, his eyes fall on the calendar, and he lets out an audible gasp. Today is Valentine's Day.

Connor decided to take a relaxing bath before getting dressed in light blue jeans, a plain white t-shirt, and a red shirt left unbuttoned. Instead of a heavy coat, he chose to wear a blue body warmer for added warmth. He spent some time styling his hair before checking the clock: it was almost 10 o'clock and he was all set.

10:00am and Clyde knocks on the door and Connor opens it with a huge smile on both of their faces,

'You ready Connor?' Clyde asks.

'Yup, ready and excited.' Connor replied.

'They both jump into Clyde's car. You sure you do not want me to drive instead as you drove last night?' Connor asks.

'No, it is ok. I love driving. When we go somewhere, you will not be doing any driving, you can just chill and relax,' Clyde answers.

'Right, ready to go?' Clyde asks.

'Oh yes, I am ready to go, but hang on for a minute. Where are we going to then?' Connor asks.

'Well, what about the zoo? That seems pretty cool for a day out on a date, do you not think?' Clyde replied.

'Yeah, that sounds really good,' Connor says.

'Let's go do that then,' Connor says.

Clyde starts the engine and heads to the zoo. As they drive, Clyde suggests that Connor turn on the music.

'I made I playlist for you. Just plug it in and click on the Connor playlist. 'Clyde says,

'Omg really, that's really nice of you to do that, but are you sure you don't want to put your music on I mean it is your car? I don't mind listening to your kind of music,' Connor says.

'No, honestly, I do not mind. That is why I have done this playlist for you,' Clyde says.

'Wow, look what you got on here, Britney, Kesha, Kelly Rowland, Girls Aloud, Dannii Minogue. Oh, I love it. You even have the Boulet Brothers on it.' Connor said.

'Yeah, well, I knew who you liked because I went through your Facebook of the artists' pages that you have liked,' Clyde shared.

'Oh, did you ok cool?' Connor says.

'Everything ok Connor?' Clyde asks,

'Everything's good,' Connor responds with a smile directed at Clyde. He could not help but think it was strange that he had gone through his Facebook page without sending a friend request. But he quickly pushes those thoughts aside as he focuses on his plans for the day: a trip to the zoo. 'It's going to be a great day and date,' he thinks, crossing his fingers in hopeful anticipation.

Connor and Clyde arrive at the zoo, and Clyde finds a spot in the packed car park to park their vehicle. It is with no surprise that it is crowded on such a hot and sunny day. They both step out of the car, and Clyde retrieves a box from the boot. Inside is a homemade lunch that Clyde had prepared for them both, which was very thoughtful of him. As they make their way towards the entrance, Clyde insists on paying for their tickets.

'No Clyde, I will pay because you drove us both here, and you got the lunch please let me pay?' Connor pleaded.

'No, I do not want you to pay for the tickets. I asked you out on this date, so I am paying for the lot. I am just so grateful you said yes to agreeing to go on this date with me. Stop worrying and just relax,' Clyde says with a big smile on his face.

'Well, thank you then. If it makes you happy, I will just relax and smile and take all your money. Just kidding about the last bit.' Connor replied.

They both start walking around the zoo and Clyde asks, 'where did you want to go to first?'

'Oh god anywhere apart from the reptile place, I hate snakes and I think I would have a heart attack if I saw some gigantic snake. Oh god just the thought of it is making my body go all weird.' Connor replied.

'Ok, that is fine. We do not have to go there. I am not a big fan of snakes either.' Clyde says.

Connor and Clyde spent approximately three hours strolling through the zoo, admiring the various animals such as monkeys, tigers, birds, zebras, hippos, and even goats. When they both felt hungry, they consulted the map to find the nearest eating area. 'There it is,' exclaimed Clyde as he pointed to a hill nearby. 'That was convenient,' remarked Connor with a smile.

'Yeah, for sure, I am knackered already.' Connor replied.

'Come on then, let's sit and eat,' Clyde says.

They both sit down to share a meal, and Clyde reaches into the box he brought with him that he had prepared earlier. He takes out sandwiches filled with smoked salmon and cream cheese, scotch eggs, a big bag of lightly salted crisps, and about ten juice boxes.

'I saw through your Instagram account that these are some of your favourites to have for lunch, so I just got them hoping to impress you.' Clyde says.

'That's really cute, thank you,' Connor says with a smile. His thoughts immediately turn to the fact that he has gone through my social media profile multiple times without adding me as a friend yet. Is that considered weird? He ponders to himself.

'Well?' Clyde says.

'Well, what?' Connor says in confusion.

'Did I impress you with the lunch I made?' Clyde asks.

'Yeah, you certainly did. Thank you it looks good,' Connor answers.

After finishing their lunch, they continue strolling through the zoo. The sun is still blazing, and Connor can feel his neck getting a bit burnt. He thinks to himself that it will sting in the shower later. As they complete a full lap around the zoo, it is already 5:15pm and they are both ready to call it quits.

'Shall we start going back now? Maybe we can go to dinner or something when we get back? Well, that is if you really want to?' Clyde asks.

'Yeah, that would be great. I'm seriously really enjoying my day with you. It's been really great,' Connor answers with a smile on his face.

As they make their way to the car, Connor reflects to himself, 'What a fantastic day, and I am exhausted. But it's not over yet, which is even better.'

Connor and Clyde start getting in the car and then drive off.

'It has been so good going out with you Connor.' Clyde says.

'Yeah, it has been a good day. I am buzzed from it,' Connor says back,

'It's getting dark now,' Connor says.

Yeah, it is. I cannot wait for it to be lighter later on in the spring, Clyde says back.

'How come there is not that many cars on the motorway? It's a bit strange. I thought we were going to get stuck in traffic on the way home so that's good that we are not,' Connor says.

'Yeah, that is good. It means I can go faster,' Clyde says.

'Well, only the speed limit.' Connor says back.

'Honestly, I am glad you have come on this date with me. I have not been on a date for ages, and I am thrilled we are doing this,' Clyde says.

'Yeah, me too. I am glad we are here today together.' Connor says back.

Clyde continues driving, and a few minutes pass in silence. Connor leans back in his seat, relishing in the events of the day. Lost in thought, he is abruptly jolted back to reality by Clyde's sudden shout.

'OH NO' Clyde shouts

'What?' Connor exclaims simultaneously with Clyde.

Clyde's grip slips from the wheel and the car hurtles towards a gnarled tree on the side of the motorway. The impact is deafening, metal crunching against wood as the car crumples like paper. Connor slumps unconscious in his seat, blood trickling down his forehead. In a panic, Clyde struggles to unbuckle his seat belt and fumble for his phone, screaming for help through trembling lips.

'Connor, Connor please wake up, wake up, PLEASE, oh no,' Clyde cries out.

Clyde fumbles for his phone, trying desperately to dial 999 as he feels a rush of adrenaline course through his veins. Suddenly, a man in dark blue jeans, a green polo shirt, and a dark blue baseball cap sprinted towards him.

'Hey man, are you ok? I have just phoned for an ambulance buddy, they will be here soon.' The Bloke says.

'Yeah, it is just my friend. He is unconscious,' Clyde says.

'He looks like he is coming to.' The Bloke says.

'Oh, thank god, Connor, Connor, can you hear me? We had a crash, but the ambulance is on its way. Don't worry,' Clyde says to Connor.

Connor wrenches his body around, fighting against the crushing force of the seatbelt. Blood trickles from a deep gash on his head, coating his face in a sticky red mask.

'Connor, are you ok?' Clyde asks.

'Yeah, I am fine. I just feel a bit drowsy, that is all.' Connor replied,

Clyde then turns to the bloke who called the ambulance and says, 'thank you for your help' and as he said that the ambulance crew has now turned up.

'No worries, the bloke said, if you are going to be ok now, I have to go, my wife is waiting for me at home.' The Bloke says.

'Yes, again thank you so much.' Clyde says.

'No worries, you take it easy now and I hope everything gets sorted with your friend and your car.' The bloke said back.

While the ambulance crew attends to Connor and Clyde, Clyde appears to be unharmed. He emerged from the car accident without any injuries.

'You will need to come to the hospital just for your head to be checked over. What's your name?' the ambulance lady asks.

'Connor' Connor replies.

'Yes, it looks like you may need a few stitches for the cut on your head,' she says to Connor.

'What happened anyway?' The ambulance lady asks.

'I was just driving, and I saw someone in the middle of the motorway,' Clyde says with Connor interrupting.

'What do you mean, you saw someone? I saw nobody in the middle of the motorway?' Connor replied.

'I swear there was someone just standing there. That is why I used the emergency break. I thought I was going to hit them.' Clyde says.

'Clyde, honestly, my eyes were in front of the road, and I didn't see anybody there.' Connor replies with a confused expression on his face.

The ambulance lady then asks, 'have you boys both been drinking?'

'No, we just come back from a day out at the zoo,' Clyde replies to her.

'Ok, well come with us and we can get your friend sorted out and then you can sort your car tomorrow,' the ambulance lady says.

They both climb into the ambulance and are quickly secured by the paramedics. As they prepare to leave, police cars arrive at the scene. The officers speak with Clyde, gathering details from him that he had already given to the ambulance team before they were to depart for the hospital.

As Clyde spoke with the police, Connor's mind raced, trying to piece together how Clyde could spot someone in the middle of a motorway. Suddenly, he felt a cold shiver course through his body, as if something more sinister and more horrific had just occurred. The police finished their questioning, leaving them both with the promise of future contact regarding the car. As the police walked away, the ambulance doors slammed shut.

Whilst in the ambulance, Connor was laying in the stretcher bed and Clyde was sitting in a chair. The ambulance lady filled out a form for Connor to give to the hospital so they can treat him faster.

They arrived at the hospital and stepped out of the ambulance, making their way to the entrance of

A&E. The hospital was a towering structure, surrounded by large glass windows that reflected the bright lights inside. Curtains were drawn in most of the windows, but the building itself seemed to radiate light. The automatic doors leading into A&E were massive, and the area was double lit as they walked inside. It was so bright that Connor had to squint for a few seconds until his eyes adjusted. Accompanied by Clyde and the paramedic, Connor approached the reception desk at A&E. The paramedic handed over Connor's information and injury sheet to the receptionist, who then asked for Connor's details for confirmation to book him in with a nurse.

'Thank you, Connor. Now, if you would like to take a seat, you are now in the system to be seen by one of our nurses.' The receptionist says.

Connor replies, 'thank you so much.'

Paramedic turns to Connor and says, Right, I am off now but you take it easy, and I hope your head heals fast.

Connor replies, 'Thank you very much for treating me and getting me here. I really appreciate that.'

'Not a problem, Connor. Both of you take care of yourselves. Bye now.' Paramedic said.

The paramedic walks off, exiting through the large automatic doors of the A&E department. As the paramedic turned a corner and disappeared from both Connor and Clyde's view, Connor notices Clyde nervously biting his lower lip.

Connor asks 'Clyde, are you ok?'

Clyde replies, 'oh yes, I am absolutely fine. Let's just get you seated and get you seen by the nurse.'

Connor and Clyde walked towards the waiting area where patients awaited their names to be called by a nurse. Connor sat motionless, but he could not help but glance over at Clyde, whose left leg was shaking uncontrollably.

'Clyde, are you really alright? You seem so anxious about something,' Connor asks.

'No, honestly, I am fine. Do you know what? I just feel so guilty that this has happened to you. I probably feel this way because really it was me that gave you that injury.' Clyde replied.

'Oh no, please don't think that way. It is fine. Everyone makes mistakes. Clyde, we will be fine.' Connor says.

'Ok, you know how to make me feel better. Thank you. Now how about I will go over to the reception desk and see how roughly it takes so that we are not sitting here not knowing if it is two hours or seven hours? Clyde asks.'

'Yeah, sure, that will be fine. No harm in asking, is there?' Connor replied.

Clyde abruptly stands from his seat, he strides purposeful as he crosses the room towards the reception desk. His body lowers over the desk as he leans in close to the receptionist, causing her to visibly tense up. As he speaks, Connor notices something off about the woman's face. It seems to be shifting, contorting into an expression of shock and fear that would go unnoticed by anyone else. But Connor's mind is on edge after his head injury and strange events of the night, so he cannot shake off this disturbing sight. Finally, Clyde straightens up and turns to make his way back to Connor's side, taking a seat beside him with a sinister glint in his eye.

'It won't be much longer now, she said. Clyde tells Connor.

After a quarter of an hour had gone by, a nurse approached Connor. This particular nurse was slender and wore a blue uniform designated for nurses. Her blonde hair was pulled tightly back into a bun, and her bright blue eyes had a warm smile that lit up the room as she made her way towards Connor.

'Would you like some pain relief?' the nurse says.

'Oh yes please, that would be great as I feel a bit of pain in my head so much that it's stinging but like a throbbing stinging,' Connor replies.

'Certainly, I have it here for you as we always get pain relief ready for someone who we can see is in pain and in need of that relief while they are waiting to be seen. We always have to ask because many people, although may not be allergic to it but they turn down pain relief.' The nurse said.

'Oh yes, I definitely am not turning down that.' Connor replied.

'Here you go then. It is liquid Oral Morphine. Open your mouth and I will squirt it in.' The Nurse asks Connor.

'There you go. That should kick in anytime soon and hopefully it won't be too much longer till you are seen by the nurse. Just let us know if you are uncomfortable or if you need anything.' The Nurse says.

'Thank you so much for your help, I will,' Connor replies.

It had been half an hour since they arrived at the emergency room for Connor's head injury to be assessed.

'Connor Summers,' a voice from a cubicle shouted.

As Connor rose from his seat, the air around him seemed to crackle with tension. The other patients in the waiting area gasped and shook their heads.

Hey, that is not fair. I have been here two hours, and he's just seen within an hour. That is not right. A patient shouted out.

'You will be seen soon. Please be patient. We are prioritising patients first to minor injuries.' The nurse replied.

Connor continued to walk to the cubicle, and Clyde also stood up to follow him and was standing behind Connor.

Connor says to Clyde 'No, it is ok. You can wait here; I will not be long. I will be fine. I could do with a cup of tea waiting for me when I get back, if that is, ok?'

'Yes, that is absolutely fine with me. I will have that ready for you. If you need me, just text me and I will come in.' Clyde says back.

'See you soon then.' Connor says.

Connor walks up to the cubicle, and the nurse in dark blue scrubs was awaiting him. From his name badge it says his name is Robin, and he was pointing at the bed.

'Hello Connor, if you could just lay on the bed for me, that would be great and then we can get you sorted.' Robin said.

'Yup, ok that is fine. I will take my shoes off, as I think they are dirty.' Connor said to Robin.

'Oh, you didn't have to do that. Most people wouldn't have thought to do that.' Robin said.

Robin had a head full of luscious black hair that framed his stunning blue eyes. His skin was flawless, and his warm smile instantly put Connor at ease before he even started the examination.

'I am now going to be touching your head and have a look at where the blood is coming from. How did this happen? I read in your notes it was a car accident?' Robins asks Connor.

'Yeah, a guy who I just started dating crashed his car. Well, I say crashed. He hit the emergency brake but the wheel kind of slipped out of his hand at the same time and we ended up sort of sliding into a tree alongside the motorway. We hit the tree on my side, so it was me that kind of felt the full force of the crash. The guy who I'm dating was absolutely fine. He doesn't have a scratch on him.' Connor replied.

'Oh god, luckily it wasn't more serious than. Why did you have to put on the emergency brake?' Robin asks.

'I'm not really too sure, Clyde. The guy I am dating said he saw somebody in the middle of the motorway, but I didn't see anybody, and I was staring right a head.' Connor replied.

'I see, so you think maybe he just thinks he saw somebody. Maybe it was a little foggy or because it was dark that he thinks he saw someone.' Robins says.

'Yeah, you might be right. Accidents happen, don't they? And I suppose this was just one of those things where something just needs to crash land into your life, just like everything else. You think things are going well, then something has to spoil it and change your entire mood just by adding some drama into your life,' Connor says.

Robin replies 'That is true. We all have to go through our difficulties, don't we? Everyone has that moment of happiness and the next thing you know; you have something come up to test you.'

'So just by going over your head you are only going to need it gluing. It will literally take me sixty seconds to do.' Robin says.

'Oh, that's great. I thought you were going to say it needed something like ten stitches.' Connor says.

'No, ok then, I'm just applying the glue now. You may feel some pressure and soreness but only for a couple of seconds.' Robin informs Connor.

Robin carefully applies the Dermabond solution onto Connor's head wound and holds it in place for a few seconds. Connor winces and takes a deep breath as Robin presses the two edges of the cut together.

'There you go. That is all done, and you are free to go. Please do not wash your hair for about three-five days. Otherwise, you will be back here getting it re-glued.' Robin says.

'Lovely. Thank you so much for that.' Connor says.

'When you are in pain, just take some Paracetamol, then two hours later take some Ibuprofen and just repeat that cycle, other than that you should be ok. Here is a leaflet of car accidents and also a head injury leaflet of aftercare from home once you leave the hospital. Take care of yourself.' Robin says.

'Thank you, Robin. You take care of yourself too, bye,' Connor replied.

'Bye,' Robin says while waving.

Connor approached the waiting area of the Emergency Room, and there was Clyde sitting in a chair. A cup of tea was placed in front of Clyde, almost as if it were waiting for Connor to come and drink it.

'Hey Clyde, I'm all done.' Connor says.

'Oh marvelous, what did they do for you?' Clyde replied.

'So, the nurse Robin, who was very friendly, he glues the cut to the head. Gave me these leaflets and just said to take some pain relief if I needed to and I am all ready to go home now.' Connor replied.

'Oh, that is fantastic. I am so glad you are ok. Here, I got you a cup of tea. It is still hot so it will be fine for you to drink.' Clyde says.

'Aww, thanks for that. This is something I really need right now, thank you.' Connor thanks Clyde.

Connor and Clyde exit the building, with Connor holding onto his cup of tea while Clyde arranges for a taxi. They stand outside the main hospital entrance. After finishing his tea, Connor tosses the cup into a nearby bin. As they wait outside the front of the hospital, Clyde spots an available taxi and signals for Connor to join him. The two of them get into the taxi and begin their journey back to Connor's house.

As the taxi arrives at Connor's house, they both exit the vehicle. Clyde hands the driver his payment and thanks him, but the driver does not say a word as he drives off before they even fully step out of the taxi.

'My gosh, he was kind of rude.' Clyde says out loud.

With his head injury and the aftermath of the accident weighing on him, Connor felt a sudden desire for company tonight. Perhaps it would be best to invite Clyde to stay over and keep him company.

Connor asks Clyde, 'would you like to come in? I don't think I can sleep yet because of my concussion.'

'Yeah, I would love to come in.' Clyde replied.

'I think I'll take a quick shower, if that's alright. I can't get my head wet because of the cut, but I'll try to wash around it to get rid of the blood. Do you want to use the shower after me? You can borrow my clothes. You could stay and watch over me in case I have any aftereffects from hitting my head,' suggested Connor.

Clyde agrees, 'That sounds perfect. I am too exhausted to go home and a shower and relaxation time with you sounds much more appealing than going back alone.'

After the boys had their showers, Connor decides to put a movie on, his favourite movie, A Nightmare on Elm Street 1984. 'Oh, I am not a big fan of horror movies' Clyde says.

'Oh really, I am. I'm like obsessed,' Connor replies.

'It is ok though, I will watch it with you.' Clyde says with a big smile on his face.

'So, are we going to talk about what you think you saw on the motorway?' Connor asks.

'Well, it is not what I think I saw. I know I saw somebody there, they were just standing there, and that is why I had to break so hard I thought I was going to hit them,' Clyde says.

'Was it a man or a woman?' Connor asks.

'I do not know; it was dark I just saw a figure.' Clyde replied.

'Maybe it was a ghost.' Connor implies.

'Don't be silly, it was not a ghost. Maybe you are right and there was no one there. I feel so bad that this has happened, and you got hurt. I am so sorry. Can we just not discuss this anymore and just watch your movie, please? I just feel so hurt and embarrassed I did that to you,' Clyde says?

'Yeah, sure, ok. That is fine, we can just watch the movie, I will not say anymore on the subject.' Connor replied.

As the movie reaches an intense part, Clyde wraps his arms tightly around Connor, pulling him in close as they both watch the movie. His fingers graze over the sensitive spot on Connor's neck, sending shivers down his spine. Throughout the entire film, Clyde keeps up this intimate gesture, causing Connor to feel safe and comforted in his embrace. By the time the credits roll, they are both fully wrapped up in each other, their bodies intertwined in a tangle of limbs and emotions. As they make their way to the bedroom, anticipation and desire fill the air between them.

Connor strides to the bed, his movements tense and purposeful. He yanks the duvet over the mattress, flinging it with force that sends pillows tumbling. With a sense of urgency, he climbs onto the bed, quickly plugging his phone into the charger before placing it on the bedside cabinet. Clyde follows suit, cautiously taking his place on the other side of the bed. Their eyes lock in an electric gaze, both feeling a surge of nervous energy coursing through their bodies. In a bold move, Clyde inches closer to Connor, wrapping his arms around him in a possessive embrace. The intensity between them is palpable as they hold each other tightly, hearts racing with desire and uncertainty about what comes next.

'This is nice being all snuggled up together after a first date.' Clyde says.

'Technically, we could say this is our third date. We could say the first one was the bar, and the second was the restaurant and this was the third date and we had a long day out together and I nearly died too. So, it has been one to remember.' Connor says.

Clyde runs his fingers over Connor's arms, causing shivers to run down his spine. They turn towards each other and begin to explore each other's lips and bodies with passionate kisses and touches. In this moment, everything feels right for them to be intimate. Together, they continue kissing as they remove their clothing piece by piece. A glance is shared between Connor and Clyde, filled with anticipation and desire. Without a word, they both understand that they are ready to take things to the next level, and they let their hands and mouths do the talking as they become intimately physical with each other.

Six Months Later

Five months ago, Connor and Clyde made the decision to move in together. They rented a private space with the goal of saving up for a future mortgage. As a result, they now have a comfortable house complete with three bedrooms, two bathrooms, and an expansive backyard. To assist them with settling into their new home, Connor's closest companion, Rex, lends a helping hand.

'Hey Clyde, are you looking forward to living with Connor? I hope you will be ok living with him.' Rex says with a sarcastic grin on his face.

'What do you mean? Course I will be ok living with him. He is amazing. Nothing bad is going to happen,' Clyde says back.

'Yeah, I know I was just bantering. I was not being serious.' Rex says.

'Yes, well, you just make sure you keep it bantering and nothing else,' Clyde says.

With a menacing glint in his eye, Clyde snatches up the box and storms away, leaving Rex reeling from the sudden escalation of what started as a harmless joke. The weight of the box that Rex was holding feels like a leaden punch to his stomach as he watches Clyde disappear around the corner, fear and confusion gripping him tightly.

'Rex, come on, get your butt in gear and put that box down,' Connor calls over.

'Yeah, just getting to it now,' Rex replied.

Rex is taken aback by the encounter he just had with Clyde. He found it puzzling because he is used to Connor's sarcastic and playful nature but was unable to handle Clyde's more serious demeanour. In hindsight, Rex should have realised this about Clyde, who tends to keep to himself and take things seriously.

The clock now reads 7:30pm and the move is complete. With Rex having left after lending a hand with moving all Connor and Clyde's belongings inside, all that remains is to unpack the numerous boxes scattered throughout the house.

'Let's just do that tomorrow. We can just have dinner, shower and then bed. I am so tired.' Connor says.

'Yes, that sounds good, well you have got the entire week off work to sort out the unpacking and making it look homely, haven't you?' Clyde says back.

'Yup, I cannot wait for everything to be sorted. Oh god our first home together, it is really exciting. It gives me butterflies in my stomach, does it you?' Connor asks.

'Of course it does. I am just as excited as you are, you gorgeous thing,' Clyde replies.

'Aww, you are so cute,' Connor says.

Connor leans over and pecks Clyde on the lips before moving to start preparing dinner.

'I'm going to get dinner ready if you want to get your shower first, Clyde?' Connor says.

'How are you going to get dinner ready when we have no shopping in?' Clyde asks.

'I got this thing called a phone and a takeaway menu. Are you mad? Did you really think I was going to be cooking?' Connor says with a smile on his face.

'I thought you were going to cook for a minute there when you said it,' Clyde says back.

'Ok, you get your shower. I will phone for a takeaway and then I will get a quick shower, then we can just sit, eat and go to bed ready for a long and busy day tomorrow,' Connor suggests.

'Ok, I will be back in a minute then.' Clyde replied.

Connor and Clyde sit down after a shower, eating their takeaway before they then decide it is time for bed. As it is going to be a long day tomorrow, unpacking and making the house look homely.

15th August

Connor and Clyde both wake up in the morning in their first home together.

Clyde heads off to work while Connor stays behind to kick off his week-long break from the care home and continue unpacking the remaining boxes. The previous day, they focused on unpacking the heavier items, leaving the rest of their belongings untouched. Today's task is sorting through books, DVDs, and other household items.

As the evening approaches, they make plans to go out for the night with Connor's friends. Clyde returns home from work, and they begin getting ready for their evening out.

'Are you ready to go out?' Connor says.

'Yup, I am ready to go,' Clyde says back.

'Ok great, let's go then as the taxi we be here any minute, it will be nice evening won't it, we have not been out for a drink with my friends for a while now,' Connor says.

'Yeah, can't wait,' Clyde replies in a sarcastic tone.

'What's the matter? Do you not like my mates?' Connor asks.

'Yes, I do, well ok I am just going to be honest. I do not like Rex.' Clyde says.

'What. are you joking? How can you not like Rex he's like my best friend ever, he is great.' Connor says?

'Yes. ok do not go overboard with the compliments, only your boyfriend you are talking to here.' Clyde says.

'Hang on a minute. I was not saying those things to make you feel like crap. It's true he has been my best friend since we were at school together, and he comes with the package with me,' Connor says.

'Yes, I know, that is why I just grit my teeth and go along with it.' Clyde says.

'But I do not know why you would have to grit your teeth with him. What has he done to make you think otherwise?' Connor asks.

'Well, I think he likes you a little more than just best friends,' Clyde says.

'Oh, get out of here, likes me more, don't be weird.'
Connor says.

'I am just saying it because that's how I sometimes
feel when he's around you,' Clyde says.

'That is just silly to think of us anything other than
best friends. It is actually just wrong. He is like my
brother, but we get that all the time with our
partners. They become a bit jealous of our
friendship,' Connor says.

'I am not jealous, you silly boy,' Clyde remarks.

'You obviously are, otherwise, you would not be
saying any of this,' Connor says.

'Taxi's here. Let's go.' Connor adds.

Without a word, both Connor and Clyde climb into
the taxi. The entire ride to the pub is spent in silence
until they reunite with their friends. Only then does
the silence break as they exchange greetings and
catch up with one another.

Susan asks, 'how's it going with the new house?'

Connor replies, 'Yeah, it is going well, thanks. I have unpacked a lot today so just got to make it ours now.'

Rex asks, 'when is the housewarming party then? Maybe I could organise it for you?'

Clyde responds, 'I will organise my house and my house party. Thank you.'

Connor says, 'Clyde, he was only joking. He meant we throw a party, and he will help set up. There is no need to bite his head off.'

Clyde says back 'I am not. Clyde turns to Rex and says, 'sorry Rex, I did not mean that. It has just been stressful these last few days, that is all.

Rex accepts Clyde's apology and says, 'it is ok, I know how stressful it is to move to a new house and anyway we are out not so we can just chill for tonight.'

Clyde says 'yes, you are right, let's just have a chilled night, shall we?'

As the night comes to an end, Connor and Clyde call for a taxi and head back to their new home. After paying for the taxi, they enter their new house, which closely resembles Connor's previous home before he moved out. The front of the house boasts a perfectly manicured lawn with bushes lining the front garden. The door is large and made of sturdy dark wood. Stepping inside, there is a staircase directly in front that leads to three bedrooms and a bathroom on the upper level. The interior of the house is painted a cool shade of grey, with black accents such as the staircase railing and skirting boards. To the right of the stairs is the living room, while the kitchen and a second bathroom are located to the left. The kitchen features white cabinets with a hint of yellow and is spacious enough to fit a dining table and chairs. In the back corner of the kitchen is a door that leads to the backyard.

Connor recognised the familiar look on Clyde's face, one that he had seen during his childhood when he got into trouble and his mother gave him a stern lecture.

Clyde says, 'you showed me up tonight sticking up for that little prick.'

Connor replies, 'what do you mean sticking up for him? You're talking about when I said that is not what he meant because it is not what he meant.'

Clyde says, 'you know what you did. I will not argue with you.'

Clyde storms up to Connor with a seething rage in his eyes, their faces inches apart. He growls through gritted teeth, 'If you ever dare to humiliate me in front of your pathetic friends again, I will make sure you pay for it.'

Clyde took a step back away from Connor's face and then Connor just froze in the same place. He was stunned and shocked. Connor's happiness over the past few days of moving into a new home, the feeling of celebrating with his now new lover. Connor sinks right into himself and felt himself getting so red that the blood has rushed over his whole body. As if a big anaconda snake just squeezed the life out of him.

Connor replies, 'ok, I am sorry. I did not mean to do that and would never do that to hurt your feelings,'

Clyde responds just so that we are clear. 'I dislike feeling like I have been told off, especially by my boyfriend.'

After calling it a night, Clyde and Connor both climb into bed. Clyde wraps his arms around Connor, holding him tightly as they drift off to sleep. But as he lays there, Connor cannot help but question whether he made the right decision. Was he overthinking things, or did he truly make a mistake? He begins to wonder if it was actually him who was at fault in the argument earlier. Finally, Connor concludes that he was indeed in the wrong for contradicting Clyde and causing embarrassment. He falls asleep feeling guilty.

Connor wakes up in the morning to find that Clyde is not in bed. Shortly after, Clyde enters the room with a tray of a freshly cooked breakfast and a glass of orange juice, along with a cup of tea.

'I thought I would just apologise for last night. I am honestly so sorry that I kind of lost my temper a little.' Clyde says.

'Oh, that's unnecessary. It's fine, really.' Connor replied.

'It is ok, I don't mind you telling me when I am in the wrong. I mean, if you cannot then who the hell can, huh?' Clyde says to Connor.

Connor replies, 'no, it is fine and thank you for doing me breakfast in bed. This is great and looks so good.'

Clyde says, 'the mail has come early today. You got three letters. They must be letters confirming that you have changed address with your bank, etc. This one is just marked with your name on it. The address is also not on it. Looks like someone hand posted it.'

Connor's eyes are drawn to the letter, and he opens it immediately. Inside is a folded piece of paper, which he carefully unfolds. The letters on the page have been cut out from a newspaper or magazine, spelling out one word: 'RUN'.

Connor looks at Clyde and says, 'did this come this morning? You didn't see who posted it, did you?'

Clyde says, 'no I did not. It was there when I went downstairs. Why does it say run? run from what?'

'I really do not know. That is actually weird, Clyde, just bin it.' Connor asks Clyde,

'Ok then, you can just forget about this. It is crap, obviously.' Clyde says, 'I have to go out so I will not be long. I Just need to go into work and sort a few things out. Do you fancy just watching a movie tonight cuddling up on the sofa?' Clyde says.

'Yeah, that will be lovely. I am staying in today. I will clean a bit of the house and unpack the last of the boxes while you are gone,' Connor says.

'Ok then, well I will see you later on tonight then, yes?' Clyde says.

'Yup, you will, bye love you.' Connor says.

Clyde replies with a 'I love you too',

They lean in towards each other and share a tender kiss. Clyde exits the room, leaving Connor with a strange sensation in his stomach. He can't shake off

Connor thinking of that bizarre letter that was slipped through the letter box. Filled with curiosity, he retrieves the letter from the bin and unfolds it once more, but the uneasy feeling in his gut persists.

He could not understand why anyone would want to harm someone mentally like that, so Connor threw it back in the bin and he pushed the thought away. Instead of dwelling on it, he decided to forget about it altogether. Connor took some time to clean up and then messaged his friend Rex to hang out, since they had gone out the previous night and did not have to work today.

(Connor) Hey Rex, what are you doing? Do you want to come over for a little while? xx

(Rex) Hey mate, yeah, sure, I am not busy. I can come over if you like. Is Clyde there? xx?

(Connor) ok cool. No, he is not here. He is at work. xx

(Rex) ok then, will be right over. xx

Rex arrives at Connor's new house and knocks on the door.

'Hey, Rex,' Connor says,

'Hey, Connor, I can't believe you now live like a ten-minute walk from me. It is nice to know you are just around the corner instead of having to travel like thirty minutes to get to you,' Rex says.

'Yeah, it is really nice. It is just like when we were thirteen and at school with living just a few minutes away from each other.' Connor says back.

'Do you mind me asking why you asked if Clyde was here? You're not uncomfortable around him, are you?' Connor asks Rex.

'No and yes, I do not know. It's just after last night he just made me feel a bit uneasy. I know we cleared it up, and it was just misheard but even before that I could feel he doesn't like me. Say if I come over to you, it's like he's watching me and just staring daggers at me,' Rex says.

Connor replies, 'no he does like you, I just think he probably has a hard time dealing with how close of a friendship we have. Don't worry, he will get used to it in time.'

'Do you want a drink? Tea?' Connor asks Rex.

'Yes please, Tea please.' Rex says back.

Connor fills the kettle and flips the switch, then begins preparing tea bags in mugs. He debates whether or not to show Rex the letter he received this morning.

'Rex, let me show you this,' Connor says.

Connor walks over to the bin and removes the letter he had received in the mail. He then presents it to him to see.

'Look at this, the envelope was handwritten in my name, and no one has got my new address apart from like banks, my work, Clyde's work, etc,' Connor says.

'What was inside then?' Rex says.

'Look, here it is. It's just got the word RUN. They have cut the letters out of a newspaper,' Connor replies.

'Wow, I don't know what to say. If your work and Clyde's work have your address, do you think anyone there could have done this as a joke?' Rex asks.

'No, there's no one there that is like that. This could be a thing to do to someone for like Halloween, April fools or something,' Connor says.

'I would just put it back in the bin and forget about it. I mean, it might not even be for you, it could be for the person who moved out before you. Someone has put through the door to scare them, but there not actually living here anymore.' Rex says with a smirk on his face.

'Don't be silly, they addressed it to me,' Connor replies.

'Oh yeah, I forgot about that bit. Sorry.' Rex says back.

Connor says, 'I will just put it back in the bin and forget about it. It was a bit creepy getting that this morning, but now the day is getting on it doesn't seem that much of a big deal.'

Rex replies, 'yup, put it in the bin and leave it there, anyway where's my bloody tea?'

Connor and Rex take a seat at the dining room table, reminiscing about their shared memories.

'I am sad that you have settled down into a relationship. I used to love your stories when you went on dates. You were funny, especially the one with the loose bowels.' Rex says.

Connor says, 'oh my god yeah, I mean, who carries on eating a dodgy pizza just because someone paid for it, then wake up in the middle of the night running to the toilet. I could not believe it. I sat on that toilet, put tissue down so he could not hear the splashing, then to top it all off, the flush did not work properly, and I had to flush five times. I just cannot believe when I went back in his bed and left the toilet door open down the hall and just lying there and suddenly, I could smell it. I was absolutely mortified. #mortified.'

Connor continues to say, 'oh well, never mind, I am with the right guy now. I just think sometimes because I have had so much bad luck with guys that this is just going to crumble at my feet.'

Rex says, 'no it won't, you just think that because you are a negative nelly. You should just be positive and think everything is going to work out.'

Rex says, 'right, I'm off then. Thank you for the tea. I got to get home and do a bit of housework.'

Connor replies, 'yeah sure, well thanks for coming round and I will just totally forget about that note that was put through the door.'

Connor walks to the door with Rex, and they embrace in their customary goodbye hug. After saying farewell, Rex departs. Connor then starts to unpack and tackle tasks before Clyde's return home.

Sitting on the sofa, Connor gazes around his new house and takes in all that he has accomplished today. His mind is buzzing with ideas for decorating and making the space his own. Suddenly, the sound of a key turning in the front door catches his attention. In walks Clyde, who immediately heads to the living room to see how much progress has been made with unpacking.

'Wow, you have been really busy. It is looking good,' Clyde says.

'It is nearly there. I just can't believe how much I have done today.' Connor replied.

'I think that deserves a takeaway. What do you think? What do you fancy?' Clyde asks.

Connor replied. 'I think a Chinese would be great,' Connor says with a big smile on his face.

With their takeaway in hand, Connor and Clyde make their way to the kitchen and sit at the dining table. The kitchen is still cluttered with boxes, but Connor plans on tackling the mess tomorrow during his day off.

Clyde looks up at Connor and asks him, 'so did anyone come round to look at the new house today?'

Connor replies, 'well yeah, Rex came round earlier for a cup of tea.'

Clyde asks, 'oh I see, and I suppose you showed him that note, yes?'

'Well yeah, of course I did. It's not a normal thing to be getting that through your door every day, plus, he's my best friend. I tell him everything.' Connor says.

'What did he say about it then?' Clyde asks Connor.

'He just said to forget about it as it could be just someone playing a silly joke as they would know I would get all paranoid about it.' Connor says.

'Yeah, well, that is what you have got to do, anyway. You need to just forget about it.' Clyde says.

'Clyde, I have forgotten about it. You're the one that brought it up in the conversation,' Clyde says.

'Yeah, alright, don't take that tone with me. I am only asking about your bloody day.' Clyde replied.

'Ok for god's sake, just leave it. Forget the note and this conversation,' Connor says.

'Ok then, well, what are you doing tomorrow then?' Clyde asks Connor.

'I am just going to sort this kitchen out.' Connor says back.

'Ok great, well, I still got work. I am sorry I am not helping.' Clyde says,

'That is ok, I really do not mind. I only got a few more days off and go back to work next week.' Connor says.

'Well, here's a thought: why don't you give up work, look after the house and not have to worry about going to work?' Clyde asks Connor.

'What? quit my job to have no job?' Connor replied.

'Yeah, that's right, I make enough money for the both of us. I got a software job's coming out of my ears and I am making a lot of money. You do not need to work.' Clyde says.

'No, sorry, but I love my job and I like to be active and go to work seeing everybody. I could never give that up, seriously?' Connor replied.

'Well, I think you should. You can look after the house, and you can be my stay-at-home house husband.' Clyde says,

'No, it's ok thank you I am fine with having my job plus doing the house. I will be absolutely fine with that. I'm not giving up my job,' Connor replies.

17th August

Connor wakes up and groans as he remembers it's his first day back at work after a week-long break. It feels like the week flew by in the blink of an eye. Already, he feels exhausted before the day has even begun. Moving into a new house is no easy feat, and Connor can still feel the strain from all the heavy lifting and unpacking. He dreads spending the whole day feeling drained and grumpy. To make things worse, he knows his coworkers will make snide remarks about how lucky he was to have time off while they were stuck working. He rolls his eyes and begrudgingly starts getting ready for his shift.

Clyde shouts up the stairs, 'WANT ME TO DROP YOU OFF?'

Connor comes to the stairs and answers back, 'yeah please, I am ready now.'

'Come on then, let's go,' Clyde says.

As they arrive at Connor's workplace, a large black gate stands in front of them. On the side of the gate is a code box where a code must be entered to gain entry to the building.

'Have a great day back at work,' Clyde says.

'Cheers, I'll see you tonight. Is it ok if you pick me up as you dropped me off? I mean, I can see if anyone can give me a lift or not?' Connor says.

'No, it is ok, I will come pick you up at 9:00pm, not a problem.' Clyde answered back.

'Yup, ok then. See you later. Have a good day,' Connor says.

'Aren't you even going to give me a kiss goodbye?' Clyde asks.

'Sorry, yeah, of course I am,' Connor says.

Before they part ways for work, Connor leans in to give Clyde a kiss on the lips. Their hands touch briefly as Connor steps back to walk towards his place of work.

Connor enters the code to the gate and walks up to the door to enter his work place. Connor turns the doorknob to enter his large, white building with a black door. He steps into the spacious hallway, lined with multiple rooms. Making his way towards the office located halfway down the hall, he prepares himself for another long day at work. As he enters the office, he is greeted by Reece Trammer, a tall and stocky man in his forties. Reece is dressed in a dark blue suit with a crisp white shirt and matching tie to his suit. He looks directly at Connor and addresses him by name.

'Morning Connor, I hope you had a wonderful week off and settled into your new home.'

'Morning Reece, yeah well, wasn't really a week off relaxing. Moving was a bit hard work, but we got there,' Connor replies.

'Well, I am sorry to burst your bubble of feeling great from moving into a new house and being back to work. I need to take you into my office with Selina and talk to you about the day just before you left for your annual leave,' Reece says.

'Ok then, what was wrong then?' Connor asks.

'Just come with us and we will explain to you,' Reece says.

Connor reluctantly accompanies Reece and Selina to his small purple office, which is sparsely furnished with only a desk, a computer, and two chairs. The walls are lined with filing cabinets that hold all of the old files. The room is also filled with various house plants, giving it a slightly cluttered but homey feel. As they all take a seat, Connor cannot help but wonder what this meeting is about.

'Connor, on the Sunday before you left your shift to begin your week off. Night staff have made an official complaint about you leaving the black gate open to the entrance of the building when they came in at 9:15pm. I mean, I do not have to explain to you the fatal consequences if someone had got out. Just because you were not being very observant in making sure the gate was shut and secured, do I?'. Reece explained to Connor.

'Hang on, that wasn't me. I left early that day, the team leader gave me permission to leave at 8:45pm. I wasn't the last one out plus you had seven other people go through that black gate at 9:00pm after me, and why was this discovered at 9:15pm if night staff come in at 9:00pm?' Connor asks.

'Well, that member of staff was late for their shift, and I was fine with their reason for that and all the staff saying it was you that left it open. It was the team leader that day has said you were the last person out that night and were meant to shut the gate,' Reece says.

'Well, of course they would because it was obviously them that did it and blaming someone else as in me just so that they did not get this telling off. I am not stupid I always remember to shut the gate because I know of the fatal consequences as you said from the gate being left open.' Connor says.

'So, are you saying it was not you, then?' Reece asks.

'Well, I did just say it was not me. I just even told you I left at 8:45pm that day. I asked the team leader if I could go early that day and they said yes. As I just said, there were seven other people that left the building through that gate fifteen minutes after I left the shift.' Connor replied.

'Well, that team leader said you were the last one to leave, you were behind them, and you were the last one out of those gates. I cannot actually defend you with this as well as it appears you did not clock out at 8:45pm. You did not clock out at all that day so can you see how this can frustrate for me? You also have to sign out of the staff book. Connor, you are in the book, and it says you signed yourself in at 6:30am but there is no signed time of you leaving the building. I have several witnesses saying it was you and only one person, which is you saying it was not you.' Reece says.

'Oh well, that's great then.' The team leader said it was me. I was in a rush to get out. I grabbed all my things and just left but I left at 8:45pm and yes, I obviously forgot to clock out and sign out in the staff book. I did not lie about leaving work early. It seems like you are accusing me of opening the gates just to mess with everyone. How dare you call me up in here, investigate me even for something I have not done,' Connor said.

'We are only investigating what actually happened and what has been reported to us,' Reece says.

'Yeah, sure, so have you investigated anyone else that could have left the gates open?' Connor asks,

'No, we have not. That is why we want your story.' Reece replied.

'I am not being funny, but it sounds like you have made your mind up and on that note. You can forget about me working here. I have had enough of just explaining myself all the time and it is obvious someone left the gate open. They were just too scared to own up but yet somehow it was me fifteen minutes after I left, I quit, and I am going home.' Connor says,

'Wait, Connor, do not do this. Just let us all figure this out. It would only probably be a writing warning on your record,' Reece says.

'IT WAS NOT ME.' 'Why can't you process that? You are telling me it was me; you weren't there, you are going on hearsay, and I am telling you it was not me. I love this place and I love working here but constantly time after time you dish out disciplinary to people when you could avoid it. You dish them out when they have not even done what has been reported, so goodbye.' Connor replied,

Connor rises from his seat and exits the office. He descends a flight of stairs and makes his way to the locker room to retrieve his personal belongings. He is well aware that it is unprofessional to abruptly leave a job without giving a two weeks' notice, but he has reached his breaking point and it's time for him to move on. The dynamics of the workplace have shifted, making it difficult to maintain perfection in his work. Neglecting the present will only hinder productivity, and besides, Clyde had assured him that their income was sufficient for both of them.

Connor begins to make his way down the hallway towards the front door. As he approaches the end of the hallway, Susan turns the corner and they come to a halt, standing in front of each other.

Susan says, 'what are you doing Connor? why do you have your bag with you?'

Connor replied, 'I just quit my job. They had accused me of leaving the gate open when I was last on shift. I endangered lives, but it was not me though. It was a little confusing, to be honest, so I just quit.'

'What are you going to do, then? What about money?' Susan says back.

'It is fine. Clyde actually said about me quitting and just staying at home. I will be a kept man.' Connor said.

'Are you sure that's going to be healthy for you? What about if you break up? I am not saying you will. It is just I do not want to see you in a dangerous situation.' Susan says.

'We will not break up. It will be fine. I get what you are saying, though. I suppose I would just have to wait and deal with that if it comes to it,' Connor replies.

'Well, you know I will support you whatever you do plus, if anything was to happen, you always have me to fall back on and I will help you in any way I can,' Susan said.

'Aw thank you, I love you. You are a part of my life. Thank you, Susan.' Connor said.

'Well, I mean it. If anything should happen, you always have a place at mine. I have got no partner and I only have my little five-year-old angel Eva and you know she loves you too bits. She would probably want you to stay in her room.' Susan says,

'Thank you so much, you really are one of the sweetest people I have ever met,' Connor replies.

Connor and Susan embraced each other with their arms wrapped around each other tightly before they pulled away to face each other.

'I will miss working with you, but I am glad I am in your life too and I won't miss anything you do next as I will always be there.' Susan says.

'I will miss you too, and you are very correct. You will not miss a thing as you will still be in my life and I will do exactly the same with you for being there for you whenever you need my support, too.' Connor says back.

'See you soon then.' Susan says.

'Speak to you soon. Bye.' Connor replied.

'Bye,' Susan says as she walked off up the hallway to go back to her work.

Upon arriving home, Connor heads straight to the kitchen and takes a seat at the dining table. He pulls out his phone and dials Rex's number, hoping he would be free to come over. Connor wants to discuss a recent decision he made and get Rex's opinion on whether it was the right one or not.

'Hey Rex, I just quit my job,' Connor says on the phone to Rex.

'Oh my god really, why did you do that?' Rex says,

'Well, if you come over, because I take it, you are off work today, I will tell you when you get to mine,' Connor says.

'Yeah, ok then. I will come over. Just give me fifteen minutes and I will be there.' Rex says.

Rex arrives at Connor's house and enters to find two cups of tea already waiting on the dining room table. As they sit and chat, Connor fills Rex in on what happened at work, and Rex expresses his disapproval for how the situation was handled.

'So, it could not have been me unless I come back fifteen minutes later, to open the gates, then go back home. Who would do that?' Connor says.

'Yeah, I can understand you getting angry and quitting, but what the hell are you going to do now?' Rex replied.

'Well, Clyde said I didn't have to work and that he earns enough money for the both of us,' Connor says.

'Wow ok, are you sure that would be the right thing to do, I mean? What would happen if you and Clyde split up? You would have nowhere to live, no job?' Rex says.

'Oh, that is fine. I mean, if anything like that was to happen, I am a care worker, and it is so easy to just get a care worker job when you have that caring experience, plus with the house part. Susan said no matter what happens, if I ever need her or a place to stay, if the future goes wrong for me, then I have always got a place to go with her.' Connor replied.

'Yeah, but are you not going to be really bored with just being at home all the time, shopping, housework, cooking, diy etc?' Rex says.

'Well, I would just have to keep coming up with different projects to keep me busy.' Connor replied.

'Well, I think you are mad, but if it's what you want to do for now, then go ahead,' Rex says with a smile on his face.

'So, have you thought anymore about that letter you got?' Rex asks.

'No, I have not to be honest. I forgot about it.' Connor replied,

'That's good then,' Rex answers.

'Right, I have got to go now, so I will see you in a couple of days or something,' Rex says.

'Yeah, sure, give me a text one day this week.'
Connor says back.

Rex and Connor stand at the door, exchanging a hug
before parting ways. As Connor watches his friend
leave, just as Rex turns away to walk towards the
path he sees a kind of frustrated expression on Rex's
face. This left Connor feeling uneasy and uncertain
what it meant.

Connor closes the door behind him and makes his
way back to the kitchen, only to find that the back
door is wide open. A chill runs down his spine as he
realizes he does not remember opening it. His
curiosity piqued; he walks over to close the door
when something catches his eye on the chair where
Rex was sitting just moments ago.

An envelope with his name scrawled across it in bold
letters sits innocently on the chair. But Connor
knows better. It is the same kind of envelope he
received the day before, filled with an eerie warning.
His hands tremble as he reaches for it, unsure of
what horrors may await inside.

Connor's trembling hand opens the mysterious package, revealing a folded piece of paper inside. As he unfolds it, his heart drops at the sight of cut out newspaper letters spelling out ' I SAID RUN'. A cold sweat breaks out on his forehead as he realizes that someone has been watching him, leaving threatening messages in the safety of his own home. His mind races with fear and paranoia, wondering if Rex was the one who opened the door or if someone else had been inside. Desperate for reassurance,

Connor decides to wait for Clyde to come home before telling him about the chilling discovery. But as he sits alone in the eerily quiet house, he cannot shake the feeling that he is being watched, and that his life may be in danger. Every creak and rustle sends shivers through him, and he cannot help but wonder. What is next.

It is now 5:30pm and Clyde walks through the front door. 'Connor?' Clyde calls out.

'Yeah, I am here in the kitchen.' Connor answers.

Clyde walks through to the kitchen and says to Connor, 'how was your day then?'

Connor answers him, 'well I quit my job. Rex came round, and I got another creepy letter.'

'What? really? show me it and wait, you quit your job too?' Clyde asks.

'Yeah, I quit my job as they accused me of something so silly and I thought about what you said to me about quitting my job, it played on my mind. It seemed like a great adventure to just quit at the time of that moment of madness.' Connor says.

'Well, do not worry, we will be fine like I said I make a bit of money so everything is good, so where is this letter?' Clyde asks.

'Here, it says 'I said run'. Don't you think that's a bit creepy, and they addressed both of the letters I have now received to me?' Connor says,

'I do not know what to say about it. It sounds creepy, but just let it go, really. Until we will get another letter and hopefully there will not be another one, but maybe go to the police if you get another one.' Clyde says.

'Rex came round, and I walked with him to the front door and when I got back into the kitchen, the back door was open, and they left this on the chair where Rex was sitting.' Connor says.

'Are you sure Rex is not the one doing it? I said that I believe he looks at you more than just a friend?' Clyde replies.

'No, he wouldn't do that, and I wish you would stop saying that it's not true. I would know by now, as we have been friends since school. He would have let something big like that slip out by now.' Connor says back.

'Well, I mean. It could be just that the door opened, or you opened the door and forgot you opened it. Look, you are safe; it is probably a joke, or someone is trying to mess with you. Just put it to the back of your mind and I will tell you what. If you get another letter, we will go to the police just to inform them to keep your mind at peace, yeah?' Clyde says.

'I am not sure. The only reason why I am questioning about putting it to the back of my mind is that it appeared in the house Clyde, and I really do not know if I opened the back door. I mean, it was unlocked but I just cannot remember if I opened it. It could have been me that opened it, but I suppose with me finding the note, I have just imagined someone opening it, came in and placed the note where Rex was sitting.' Connor replied.

'I know it is going to be hard to shut this off from your mind, but to be honest, there is nothing we can do. If we get another note. We will both go to the police just to make them aware of these notes and possibly someone coming into the house to leave them. That way they might put you on record, so if anything was to happen, then they would prioritise coming here. Clyde says back.

It is now the next day and as the morning light begins to seep through the curtains, Connor rises from his bed and makes his way to the window. He gazes out at the front garden, a sense of unease creeping over him like a thick fog. His heart races as he recalls the disturbing letters that were hand-delivered to his new home. How did this person know where he lived? Is it some sick joke or a cruel mind game? The thought of someone toying with his emotions sends shivers down his spine. It is not just unsettling, it is downright cruel. Playing with someone's mental health in this way is sickening and reprehensible. Connor can feel the weight of fear pressing down on him, suffocating him with every breath.

Connor makes his way to the wardrobe, already planning to take a shower later since he has no plans for the day. He opens the wardrobe and pulls out a pair of black jogging bottoms with a white stripe down each leg. Next, he chooses a black T-shirt and grabs a matching black hoodie. The hoodie also has white stripes running down the arms. After getting dressed, Connor heads downstairs to start unpacking more boxes.

Throughout the day, Connor busies himself with tidying up the house and finally getting around to unpacking the remaining boxes. It helps to distract him from his thoughts, until a text message from Clyde comes through at 6:00pm.

(Clyde) Hey Connor, I am sorry, but I have to work all night on this new software I am doing. So, I must spend the night in my office doing the work and will not be home until tomorrow morning. xx

(Connor) Oh god, really? Ok that is not a problem. I will have to just get an early night then. Hope the night goes quick for you and you sort out the software. XX.

(Clyde) Thank you, I will be home tomorrow as soon as I can. Love you. xx

(Connor) Love you too. xx

As Connor's mind reels with thoughts of the creepy letters and the absence of Clyde, his heart races with panic. He cannot bear to spend the night alone, but he also does not want to burden anyone else by asking for a place to stay. Frantically, he grabs his phone and texts Rex, hoping that his friend will agree to keep him company through this terrifying ordeal.

(Connor) Hey Rex, are you busy tonight? Clyde is not coming home from work and wondered if you wanted to stay the night? xx

(Rex) Hey Buddy, I am sorry I can't do tonight as I do not finish work till 9:00pm and I got to be up at 5:00am as I start work again at 6:00am, sorry. xx

(Connor) That's ok not to worry. Hope the shift goes alright for you tomorrow. xx

(Rex) oh god, I hope it goes quick. xx

The clock reads 10:00pm, signalling the end of another long day for Connor. With a tired sigh, he locks all the doors and trudges upstairs to his bedroom. The hallway is dimly lit, casting shadows on the walls and floor. In his room, the only source of light comes from his phone as he lays in bed. His fingers scroll mechanically through social media feeds, but gradually his eyes start to droop. He sets his phone on the bedside table and finally gives in to sleep, pulling the covers up to his chin. As he drifts off, thoughts of the two letters that he had received swirl in his mind. But he pushes that aside, reminding himself that morning will come and with it, Clyde's return. Just as he begins to enter a deep slumber, a loud knock at the door jolts him awake.

Suddenly jolted awake, Connor sits up in bed and checks his phone. The glaring numbers read 11:30pm. 'What the hell,' he mutters to himself. He descends the stairs cautiously, taking each step carefully. Just as he reaches the halfway point, a loud knock echoes through the house once again.

As Connor reaches the door, a gut-wrenching feeling fills his stomach. He hesitates to speak, but after a tense ten seconds, he finally asks, 'Who is it?' Instead of a human voice, a demonic growl echoes through the door, causing Connor's blood to run cold. 'Why haven't you run?', the voice taunts with an otherworldly tone that chills Connor's bones and sends him scrambling for safety.

Connor's heart hammers relentlessly in his chest, fear gripping him in a vice-like grip as he stares at the door. He cannot shake the feeling that the person on the other side of the door is the one behind the threatening letters, urging him to run for his life.

Temptation to open the door floods through him, but he cannot erase the images of horror movies where the first person who investigates always ends up dead. Sweat beads on his forehead as he stands frozen in terror, unsure of what lies beyond the threshold.

'GO AWAY, I am going to call the police,' Connor says to the mysterious person.

Connor rushes into the living area and slowly pulls open the curtains, revealing a shadowy figure lingering just beyond the bushes. In an instant, the figure disappears into the pitch-black night. With trembling hands, Connor grabs a baseball bat and positions himself on the staircase, ready to defend himself against any potential threat. Adrenaline courses through him, keeping him alert and wired all night long. Exhaustion is a foreign concept as fear consumes his every thought and action.

At 8:30am, Clyde entered through the front door after unlocking the door with a key. Connor immediately stood up and recounted what had happened. After hearing the story, Clyde determined that they needed to go to the police and report it.

The clock read 9:30am as Connor and Clyde arrived at the police station in Southport. The path leading up to the building was lined with neatly trimmed bushes, their greenery a stark contrast against the concrete and metal of the modern structure. The building itself was tall and seemingly brand new, its glass windows gleaming in the morning sun.

As they walked up the path, they passed by a black metal railing on the right side, separating them from a perfectly manicured grass lawn. The verdant expanse seemed almost out of place next to the intimidating facade of the police station.

Finally reaching the entrance, they were greeted by automatic doors that swooshes open before them. Stepping inside, they were met with a sleek reception area. A polished desk stood at the centre, manned by a uniformed officer who glanced up at their arrival. Connor and Clyde approached, ready to begin to ask for help.

The reception desk gleamed in the sunlight; its smooth surface made of light-coloured wood that seemed to glow. The walls were a calming shade of blue, adding to the tranquil atmosphere of the room. On top of the desk sat a visitors' book, inviting guests to leave their mark, and next to it was a striking plant. Its leaves were dark green, with small red veins running through them, and at the centre sat a curious Venus flytrap. Connor and Clyde stood behind the desk, both attentive and ready to reveal their story.

Connor nervously approaches the officer, his voice low and urgent. 'I believe I'm being stalked by someone,' he says, concern evident in his tone.

The police officer stood tall and imposing, his all-black police uniform crisp and tailored to fit his stocky build. Perched atop his head was a traditional police officer hat, adding an air of authority to his appearance. His strong jawline was adorned with a slight stubble, giving him a rugged edge. His dark brown eyes seemed to hold years of experience and wisdom as he surveyed his surroundings with a stern gaze.

The police officer responds, 'All right, let's step into this small office and you can give me more details about what's going on.'

As Connor, Clyde, and the police officer stepped into a small, cramped office. A lone desk sat in the centre, cluttered with papers and files, while a computer hummed quietly in the corner. A colourful vase of fresh flowers stood proudly on the desk, adding a touch of life to an otherwise mundane space. The three of them took their seats, forming a serious and determined circle. Clearing their throats, they launched into their explanation of events.

'My name is Randy Tuff, so nice to meet you. I am just going to jot down anything you say in my notebook if that is ok?' Randy Tuff asks.

'Yeah, of course, that is fine. I am Connor and this is my partner, Clyde.' Connor replies.

Connor then shares all the information from the notes he received with Randy Tuff.

As Connor held the two letters in his hands, he could not help but wonder about the sender. They clearly knew his address, but he never expected them to show up at his door. Especially not at 11:30 pm.

Randy Tuff replies, 'well, did you ask this person who it was?'

Connor replies, 'yes, of course, but that only thing they said to me was 'why haven't you run?'

With a sceptical look, Randy Tuff shook his head. 'I can't offer any help if I don't know who this person is,' he replied curtly. His eyes narrowed as he thoughtfully considered the situation. 'But I do have some general safety precautions for you,' he continued, his voice tense with concern. 'Get an alarm system, post warning signs about a vicious dog on your property and always be on high alert.' His expression darkened as he added, 'You never know what kind of danger could be lurking out there.'

'So really, that's the only thing that can actually happen is if I try to protect myself. What about a gun?' Connor asks.

'Well, that isn't really going to improve the situation. Having a gun is illegal. Owning a gun in the house just opens it up to possibilities of dangerous outcomes so I actually would not advise you on getting a gun.' Randy Tuff answers.

'So, if they come near me, I can wave the alarm system instructions it at them, maybe throw it at the person and pray they get a paper cut from it. Seen as that would only be my protection,' Connor says to the Randy Tuff.

'I know it can be frustrating, but that is how it happens; you could not prove that this person is stalking you and even if you find out who the person is. Unless there is physical contact or advanced threats with proof, there is not much that would be in place to be able to help you,' Randy Tuff says.

'Ok, yes. I get that. I am sorry, I am just upset and frustrated and tired even as I haven't slept all night because of this person. I was just so scared that they would come back that I sat at the bottom of the stairs until my partner Clyde came home. Look, I understand what you are saying, and I am sorry I was slightly snappy to you,' Connor says to Randy Tuff.

'It is fine. I completely understand. It must have been a horrible feeling to be that scared that you could not even sleep. Just try to take my advice on the alarm system or you could even put a sign on your front lawn showing that the house has an alarm system. If anything else happens, you are more than welcome to come back here and get more advice. You can just ask for me at the desk if I am not there.' Randy Tuff says.

'Ok then, thank you for your help and advice and if anything, else happens, believe me, you will see me again.' Connor says back to Randy Tuff.

Connor and Clyde believed that involving the authorities would be fruitless unless a significant event transpired, so they departed from the office and police station.

As Connor ponders the possibility of someone lurking around his house at night, he realises that he and Clyde need to take measures to protect themselves. Was it just a coincidence that the one night he was alone in the house, this thought crosses his mind?

Connor and Clyde returned to their home. As they walked up the narrow path towards the front door, Connor took the lead with Clyde following closely behind. On the top step leading into the house, Rex was sitting patiently, waiting for them to come home.

'Oh, hello Rex, you, ok?' Connor says.

'Yeah, I am fine. I just thought I would come and see you, see how you were after I couldn't come over last night.' Rex says.

'It was awful. I had someone banging on the door at 11:30pm and when I asked who it was, all they said was 'Why haven't you run?' That is what the person asked me. It was so creepy and by the time I got to the window to see who it was, they had already started walking off and all I saw was a dark figure disappear near the bushes.' Connor replied.

'Oh my god, really? That's so creepy. I am so sorry that I couldn't be here. Honestly, I feel bad now that you had to go through that alone.' Rex replied.

'No, it's fine now, I mean. I do not feel fine, but I feel better knowing that tonight Clyde would be with me. I ended up sitting at the bottom of the stairs all night holding a baseball bat until he got home. Anyway, I thought you were at work. You said you started at 6:00am.' Connor says.

'My manager asked me to cover a shift, but when I arrived, they said they did not need me because the other person came in. So, I am here now.' Rex says.

'Well, that was a bonus then. Come in and I will tell you about what the police said to me,' Connor asks.

'Oh, you went to the police. Ok cool, I will come in and you can tell me about it over a cup of tea,' Rex says.

Rex looks over at Clyde and says, 'oh sorry, hi Clyde.'

'Hi Rex,' Clyde says back.

Connor, Clyde, and Rex enter the house, with Rex heading straight to the kitchen and taking a seat at the dining table.

Connor glances at Clyde, who is positioned at the bottom of the stairs by the front door. 'You don't mind if Rex comes in, do you?' he asks.

'Oh yes, of course I don't mind. I am going to leave you boys to it, though. I will go upstairs. Maybe have a lay down for a bit,' Clyde says back.

'Ok, that's fine. I will see you in a bit then.' Connor says.

Clyde ascends the stairs as Connor heads to the kitchen to join Rex, who is already seated at the dining table. After making tea for both of them,

Connor takes a seat next to Rex. They discuss their recent trip to the police station, but unfortunately, there was not enough evidence for any action to be taken and nothing significant occurred.

Rex advised Connor to follow the police's recommendation and set up an alarm system as well as some obvious deterrents to discourage potential intruders. This would lessen the likelihood of successfully trespassing without being caught by the authorities.

Once they had both finished their cups of tea, Connor and Rex exchanged goodbyes at the door. As Rex made his way down the small pathway to the public footpath, Connor closed the door behind him and went upstairs to check on Clyde in the bedroom.

'Clyde, are you ok?' Connor asks.

'Yes, I am just laying down on the bed, just resting my eyes.' Clyde says.

'Ok cool, I am just going to be downstairs if you need anything,' Connor says.

'Ok, thank you. See you in a bit,' Clyde says back.

Two Months Later

30th October

The Night Before HalloweeN

Two months have passed, and nothing significant has occurred since the mysterious notes and the Menacing person at the door. Connor and Clyde have adjusted to their new home and are going about their daily lives. With halloween quickly approaching, they are excited to throw a party to celebrate. This time of year, is one of Connor's favourites, and he loves participating in various activities such as carving pumpkins, watching scary movies, decorating his house, and handing out candy to trick-or-treaters.

Connor and Clyde are dressing up as zombies for halloween. They bought have planned the outfits, ripped clothes, latex, fake blood, and red contacts.

While Clyde is busy at work, Connor takes the lead in preparing for tomorrow night's Halloween party. He enlists Susan to assist him, knowing that if he had asked Rex, they would inevitably get sidetracked and not accomplish anything.

A knock interrupts the silence, prompting Connor to make his way to the front door. He turns the knob and opens it, revealing a smiling Susan on the other side.

'Hi, Connor. I hope you're ready to get cracking. I've been looking forward to coming and help you decorate today.' Susan said.

'Hi, Susan. Come in, thank you for coming round to help me. I have everything we need to set up. I actually think I went over the top and purchased too much stuff.' Connor said.

'Oh no, don't worry about that. We will make everything look good and fit all what you got somewhere.' Susan replied.

Since the stalking incident, Connor had become a bit of a hermit and only ventured outside when absolutely necessary. Clyde offered support to help him deal with the threatening letters, but any unexpected visitors still caused him great anxiety. In an attempt to move on from the past, Connor is now decorating his home in anticipation for a halloween party tomorrow, with the assistance of his friend Susan.

Connor is relieved now that the stalker situation has
ended and there has been no further communication.
Connor feels at ease now that the stalker incident
has ceased and there have been no more attempts to
contact him.

Susan says, 'Have you been looking for a job at all,
Connor?'

Connor replies, 'Not at the moment or for a little
while, to be honest, I am pretty happy with what I
am doing at the moment. Clyde has been great, and I
am enjoying what I have.'

'Do you not feel that you are just doing the same
thing every day? I worry you may become too much
used to your own company that finding a job or
going somewhere may become a bit of a challenge
for you.' Susan Says.

Connor reassures Susan 'I'll be alright. I know I've
been keeping to myself lately, but once I feel like I'm
in a better place, I might start considering other job
opportunities outside of caregiving. And don't
worry, we have a party tomorrow night and we are
going to have a real good time together.'

'That is good. I didn't mean to pry I was just worried about you, but I am glad that you got it under control.' Susan says back.

'Yes, I promise you. I have and I will be fine.' Connor says.

'I remember having people check in on me when my husband died. I started cutting off and pushing people away, but the surrounding people helped me see that asking for help is the most adult thing you could do.' Susan says,

'Yeah, you are very right. Eva is so lucky to have a mother like you,' Connor says to Susan.

'I don't know what I would ever do if something happened to her or me even. I feel lucky every day that I have a little angel like her.' Susan responds.

The house is all set for the halloween party tomorrow night, thanks to Connor and Susan's impeccable decorating skills. With everything in place, Susan heads home while Connor takes some time to relax before Clyde returns.

Connor and Clyde had decided to spend a cozy, relaxing night in together watching horror movies.

As soon as Clyde got home, they both changed into their pyjamas and made their way to the living area. They were planning to start off with the classic HalloweeN I & II for their movie marathon.

While watching the first movie, they see Jamie Lee Curtis searching for her friend Lynda, after receiving a creepy phone call and going to a house where the shape is waiting.

Urgency grips Connor's bladder as he rushes upstairs to the bathroom. As he passes their bedroom, a strange vibrating sound emanates from the wardrobe, pulling him in to the bedroom. Curiosity gets the best of him, and he cautiously approaches the source of the noise. With Clyde downstairs, what could possibly go wrong? But as soon as he opens the wardrobe doors, the vibrating intensifies and seems to be coming from beneath the floorboards. Connor frantically moves boxes aside until he uncovers a loose floorboard. Without hesitation, he pries it open to reveal a small rusty metal box with a tiny padlock. Fear creeps in as Connor questions its origin, was it there before they moved in, or does it belong to Clyde? Unable to shake off his unease, Connor rushes to the bathroom and then heads back downstairs to watch the horror movie with Clyde, but his mind is consumed with thoughts of the mysterious box and what secrets it may hold.

Connor considers whether to inform Clyde about the box or explore it himself when he is not around. Ultimately, he chooses to wait until Clyde is at work before opening the box and revealing its contents.

HalloweeN

<u>31st October</u>

As the day of the halloween party dawns, Connor's mind is still consumed with the small box he discovered under the floorboards. He has to wait for Clyde to leave for work before he can even think about opening it.

Clyde gets dressed and is now ready to go to work.

'I am off to work now Connor, I will be back about 4:00pm to help you set up for our first party together.' Clyde says.

Connor replies, 'Ok then, that will be great, and I am so excited about it. Have a good day at work.'

'I will see you later. Love you.' Clyde says.

'Love you too,' Connor replies.

With Clyde gone and the coast clear, Connor wastes no time in executing his plan to open the mysterious box hidden under the floorboards. He grabs a paper clip, his heart racing with anticipation as he approaches his bedroom, opens the doors to his wardrobe and moves aside heavy boxes to reveal the floorboard. His hands shaking, he pries the floorboard open and extracts the box, determined to uncover its secrets. Sweat appears on his forehead as he struggles to pick the lock with the paper clip, his frustration mounting as it proves more challenging than he initially thought. But he refuses to give up, determined to unravel the truth within that little box.

Fingers trembling, Connor pries open the rusted padlock, revealing a collection of items inside. An old black flip phone, several unmarked medicine boxes, and a certificate for the Southport Psychiatric Unit are all carefully arranged. As Connor reads the name on the medication and admission certificate - Mr Victor Sharp - a wave of unease washes over him. 'Who the hell is this, Victor Sharp?' He voices his thoughts aloud as the gingerly flips open the phone to find it flooded with twenty-seven missed calls from a Dr Starbuck. His heart races as he clicks on one of the voice messages and hears the frantic voice on the other end scream, 'Victor, please pick up! It's urgent!'

'Victor, it's Dr. Starbuck again. I need you to reach out to me as soon as possible. It has been seven months without any contact from you. If you do not check in, the police will have to come looking for you. It is important for your safety and the safety of those around you that we know where you are and that you continue your treatment. Please get in touch with me.'

Connor's hands shake as he snaps a photo of the contents in the box, his heart racing with both excitement and fear. He carefully locks the box back up, meticulously placing everything exactly as he found it. But his mind is consumed with questions: what did he just stumble upon? Who is this mysterious person? Determination sets in as Connor vows to uncover the truth behind this enigmatic find, no matter the cost.

Connor realizes it is time to start preparing and adding the final details to the party. He hangs up more decorations and also prepares delicious food for his guests. As he sets the mood with halloween music, he tries to push aside any thoughts of the strange incident until he can properly investigate it. Suddenly, the front door opens, and Clyde enters, interrupting Connor's preparations.

'Oh, hey Clyde, what are you doing back so early? It's 1:00pm.' Connor asks.

'I came home early as I got my work done pretty quick today,' Clyde answers.

'Oh, that is good then. I am pleased you finished earlier; means we can do more for the party together.' Connor says.

Clyde answers back 'We sure can, I just need to get changed first".

Clyde headed upstairs to change while Connor stayed downstairs, busying himself with preparing more food for the party. Suddenly, his mind went back to the box he had seen earlier, and he became concerned if it belonged to Clyde. Why have I not asked him about it yet? A sense of unease crept over Connor as he made his way upstairs, where he found Clyde sitting next to the wardrobe with a vacant look on his face, still dressed in his clothes from earlier.

'Clyde? CLYDE?' Connor shouts out to him.

Clyde answers back 'Yes?'

'Are you ok? You look like you just been told bad news or something,' Connor asks.

'No, not bad news. I just need to go somewhere.' Clyde replied.

'What do you mean, go somewhere?' Connor asks him.

'Just somewhere. I need to go and sort something out. You... you stay here, everything will be alright.... everything's going to be alright.' Clyde says.

Clyde's gaze pierces through Connor, as if he were nothing more than a ghostly apparition. He moves towards the bedroom door with an eerie calmness. As he passes by Connor, his expression remains blank and vacant, as if his entire being is hollowed out, devoid of any emotion or humanity. The chilling emptiness emanating from him sends shivers down Connor's spine.

Clyde walks down the stairs, his footsteps echoing through the house as he walks towards the front door. Connor stands in the bedroom, his jaw hanging open in disbelief at the chaotic scene that just unfolded before him. His mind races with questions: 'What is happening? Why is Clyde behaving like this? Could it be because of that box?'

Connor's eyes scan the wardrobe frantically, searching for any sign of movement or disturbance. But everything appears untouched and in its proper place. Doubt creeps into his mind - could that box really be his? And even if it is, how could he have possibly hidden himself inside and rearranged everything so quickly? A shiver runs down his spine as he considers the implications of this unsettling thought.

Connor's mind races with conflicting thoughts. If the box is truly his, then every word Clyde has said has been a lie. And if it is not his, then why did Clyde act so suspiciously? Fuelled by determination and confusion, Connor desperately sends a text to Rex to come over immediately, determined to get to the bottom of this situation.

(Connor) Hey Rex, is it possible that you could come round earlier? There's something I need to discuss with you about Clyde? xx

(Rex) Of course I can. I am ready now anyway, so I will see you soon. xx

(Connor) Thank you. See you in a minute. xx

Connor unlocks the door and sees Rex waiting
outside. The two of them make their way to the
kitchen, where Connor shares his discovery of the
hidden items in the wardrobe and floorboard. He
also mentions Clyde's sudden departure without
explanation. Rex suggests that if they can connect
the box to Clyde, it could mean he is lying about his
identity or that the box was left there by previous
occupants. These are thoughts that have already
crossed Connor's mind.

The clock strikes 8:00pm and the guests begin to
trickle in for the party. It is clear that everyone has
put in a lot of effort to dress up, with one guy
rocking a Freddy Krueger costume and a woman
pulling off the joker look from Batman.

Arriving at the party, Susan is decked out in full
witch attire with a long black wig, green face paint, a
prosthetic warty nose, and fake claws on her fingers.
Completing her costume, she carries a broomstick in
hand.

'Alright Connor, where's Clyde?' Susan asks.

'Oh, he's had to pop out and get something. He should be back soon, though.' Connor replied.

'Oh, ok cool, I will look forward to having a chat with him then.' Susan says.

'He will be here soon, and you can chat to him as much as you like. He won't know many people, so you will make him feel at ease,' Connor says.

'Are you sure you are, ok? You look a bit like you aren't here.' Susan asks.

'No, I'm absolutely fine. I was just thinking about when I should crack open the cocktails.' Connor says back.

'Ok then, that's fine. You know if you do ever want to talk, I'm always here for you but you better hurry with them cocktails.' Susan says.

'You look good as a witch. Shame you didn't do your face up, though.' Connor says.

'How dare you! You look good as a zombie. How did you do the latex on your face?' Susan asks.

'Oh, it was actually quite simple. I looked it up on YouTube for zombie latex make up videos; they are pretty handy and simple to follow.' Connor replied.

Susan wanders off to grab a drink and mingle with the other guests. Meanwhile, Connor stands and scans the room for Rex, who seems to have disappeared since more people arrived at the party. Despite everyone who said they would come now being in attendance, Rex is still nowhere to be found. As he searches for Rex, Connor engages in small talk with partygoers who keep offering him drinks and questioning his knowledge of Clyde's whereabouts. Despite putting on a smile, Connor can feel himself getting tired from all the socializing.

The clock strikes 10:30pm and Connor cautiously steps into the dimly lit hallway, he approaches the front door. Suddenly, it swings open with a loud creak and in walks Clyde. But this is not the same Clyde that Connor knows. He is wearing a grotesque costume, his clothes torn and stained with blood. His hair is dishevelled, and he appears to have a bruised, black eye on one side of his face. A chill races down Connor's spine as he realizes that something is very wrong with Clyde, and he braces himself for whatever horror lies ahead.

'Clyde? Where the hell have you been?' Connor asks.

'I am sorry. I had to do something,' Clyde says.

'You had to do something? You left with no explanation of where you were going. I didn't know how long you were going to be. Everyone's here at the party asking where you are,' Connor says.

'I am so sorry to have worried you. Honestly, I am.' Clyde says.

'Well, where did you go? How come you have ruined your clothes? You could have just come home and warn them clothes that we have already put the rips and blood on.' Connor asks.

Clyde justifies his sudden appearance, saying, 'I did not want to disappoint you. I had to show up in something, didn't I? It was important for me to visit my family. You see, when you found me, I had just received a call about the passing of my aunt. That is why I reacted the way I did.'

'OH, I am so sorry that your auntie has passed, really sorry to hear that. It's not nice when someone dies and now I know why you acted the way you did,' Connor says.

'It is fine. She was ill, and we all knew this was coming, but it is still hard to hear that the person you knew has now gone. Anyway, no more talking about this let's just enjoy the party and we can talk about it tomorrow.' Clyde asks.

'Yeah, of course.' Connor replied.

Clyde strolls into the kitchen, helping himself to a drink and engaging in conversation with the other guests. Meanwhile, Connor steps out into the garden to find Rex already there, surrounded by a group of people.

'Rex, where have you been?' Connor asks.

'What? I've been out here,' Rex replies.

'For the last two hours?' Connor asks.

'Yeah, well, I have been out here chatting with people for a while now.' Rex replies

'Clyde's home. He went off because his auntie died.' Connor says.

'So why didn't he just tell you that?' Rex asks.

'Some people deal with grief in lots of different ways. He said we can talk about it tomorrow, Still don't explain the box, though,' Connor replies.

'No, it doesn't. What are you going to do?' Rex asks.

'I don't know what to do yet. What can I do while I wait to speak with him? All I really want is to discuss the contents of the box. But what if it belongs to him?' Connor responds.

'Why don't you look up that Dr's name? What was it Starbucks?' Rex asks?

'Dr Starbuck'. Connor replied.

As Connor uses his phone to search for Dr. Starbuck. After typing in the name, the search engine suggested a result that showed a profile linked to the Southport Psychiatric Unit. According to the information, Dr. Starbuck had been working there for a solid thirty years. Connor's heart froze as he clicked on the news, his blood turning to ice as he reads the headline: 'Dr Starbuck Found Dead, Brutally Murdered' this was published thirty minutes a go. His vision blurred as he tried to comprehend the horror of the situation. A wave of nausea washed over him when he saw the description of the murder. Forty three stab wounds to the neck, face, back and chest, a savage attack that left no doubt of the killer's intent to inflict maximum pain and suffering. Slowly, he turned to look at Rex, who had already seen it and was staring back in shock. Their eyes met and they both turned their heads toward the kitchen window to see Clyde, who stood in the kitchen with a disturbingly wide grin on his face, waving at them. It took all of their willpower not to succumb to panic and fear, instead forcing themselves to smile and wave back at him, trying to hide their true emotions.

'Oh my god, what are you going to do?' Rex asks.

'This doesn't say that he killed him.' Connor replied.

'Well, there is a hell of a lot of evidence, don't you think? The box with Dr Starbuck's name in it. After leaving earlier and returning with his clothes ripped and bloody, they have now discovered the body of Dr Starbuck.' Rex says.

'Oh fuck, what am I going to do.... no....no this can't be him, it's not him, don't forget if we are wrong about what you are saying, and it is not him then I could lose everything.' Connor says.

'And if he is a homicidal maniac, you could lose everything, like your life,' Rex says.

'Oh, you're being very dramatic. I will talk to him tomorrow. I bet you there's a perfectly good explanation for all of this,' Connor says.

'You want to hope there is for your sake?' Rex replies.

As the clock strikes 1:00pm, everyone has left the party for the night. Connor is in no condition to clean up, having been drinking alcohol. After such an exhausting day, they both decide to tackle the mess tomorrow. Connor and Clyde remove their costumes and wash off all of their makeup before getting into bed. As Connor turns to Clyde, he notices that his left black eye makeup did not come off completely during washing.

'Is that a real black eye?' Connor asks.

'Oh yeah, I walked into a shelf at the shop. You should have seen people. One lady asked if I was ok while the shop assistant laughed his arse off.' Clyde says.

'Oh, right, you walked into a shelf,' Connor says.

'Yeah, that is what I said.' Clyde says back.

'Ok, fair enough. I hope it gets better tomorrow. Again, I am sorry about your auntie,' Connor says.

'That is ok, there is no need to be sorry, just let me cuddle you all night.' Clyde asks.

Clyde shifts his body and wraps his arm around Connor, snuggling close and whispering in his ear. 'Goodnight.'

The Night After HalloweeN

The following morning, they both wake up to find Clyde's arms still tightly wrapped around Connor.

'Morning sleepy head, you ok?' Clyde asks.

'Yeah, I'm ok thank you. How are you feeling?' Connor replies

'I am ok thank you. I had a really good night's sleep, though.' says Clyde.

'Did you? That's good then. I am glad you did,' Connor replies.

Connor and Clyde woke up and get prepared for the day ahead. They spent the morning cleaning up after their first party together in their new house. Luckily, their friends and guests had been considerate and left the house in decent condition. It mainly involved washing and putting away dishes, tidying up, and packing away all the halloween decorations. As they were finishing up, Connor brought up the news of Dr. Starbuck's death from the previous night and observed Clyde's reaction closely.

'Did you hear about some Dr Starbuck? He was killed last night. Apparently, he was stabbed forty three times,' Connor says.

'Oh goodness, that does not sound good, does it, poor guy? When did you hear about that?' Clyde replies

'Last night, his daughter found him in his home.' Connor says.

'Aww, that is really sad. So much murder and evil in this world isn't there,' Clyde replies.

Connor reflects that there was not a noticeable absence of panic or fear on Clyde's expression. It was as if he had no emotional connection to the Doctor and his daughter, who had found his lifeless body.

'Will you come with me to my auntie's funeral?' Clyde asks.

'Of course I can. When is it?' Connor replies

'It is in a weeks' time, well that is what my family are aiming for anyway,' Clyde replies.

'Yeah, sure, that is fine. I will come with you. How come you have never introduced me to your family or friends? You say nothing about them, which is strange, as you must have been in contact with them to know your auntie was ill and dying. How come you have never set up a day where we could all meet?' Connor asks.

'I do not really get on with my family enough for me to introduce you to them. I never see them,' Clyde says.

'What about your friends then?' Connor asks.

'We sort of have drifted apart from each other, really.' Clyde replied.

'But wouldn't you like to reconnect with them?' Connor asks.

'JUST DROP IT' Clyde shouts

'OK, bloody hell, I was only asking questions about your family and friends I'm not asking you to take me around the world,' Connor replies.

Clyde's face contorts with a fiery rage as Connor continues to question him. He jumps up from his seat and storms off, his footsteps pounding against the floor like thunder. With a scowl on his face, he ascends the stairs like a wounded animal seeking solace in isolation. Connor is baffled by the complexity of Clyde's life, a house, a lover, and a separate family, all shrouded in secrecy.

Connor is relieved to know that he was telling the truth about his aunt, especially now that they will both be attending her funeral. However, he cannot help feeling uneasy about meeting Clyde's family for the first time in such a sombre setting, where he will not have much opportunity to speak with them and can only offer his condolences. He knows he will be a stranger amongst them, just a background observer.

Connor intends to send a message to Rex, clarifying that he had no connection to the box or Dr. Starbuck, as he was saying goodbye to his dying aunt at the time. This means he was in the company of his relatives at the time of the crime.

(Connor) Hi Rex, I wanted to update you that Clyde has invited me to attend his aunt's funeral with him. I believe he was telling the truth about being with family last night, as he also mentioned going to a shop where he accidentally hit a shelf and ended up with a black eye. xx

(Rex) Sounds a little weird to me but I am satisfied if you have had a chat with him and now attending his aunties' funeral with him.
Hopefully, this box is just nothing to do with you or Clyde and just belongs to someone else who lived in that house. xx

(Connor) That's probably what it is. I've only been with him for 8 months, but I can't imagine him being anything other than a kind and gentle person. He's like a harmless kitten to me. xx

(Rex) I am happy for you; I hope it is just us being silly. xx

Connor pushes all doubts out of his mind. He knows Clyde is kind and incapable of lying or causing harm to anyone. Connor begins to feel remorseful for even considering these thoughts. How could he have such cruel thoughts towards his boyfriend while also dealing with the grief of his aunt's passing?

Connor makes a plan for a day out with Clyde, wanting to relive the joy and chemistry they share when they're together. They have always enjoyed each other's company and cherish their time spent together.

They both discuss what activities they could do for the day. They considered going shopping, visiting the pier, or taking a leisurely stroll in the park. Ultimately, they settled on spending the day at a nearby country park, where they could enjoy nature and have meaningful conversations. Clyde had been avoiding talking about his emotions and family since his aunt's passing, but Connor tried to broach the subject only to be shut down by Clyde.

They exit the house together and make their way to Clyde's car. They're heading out to a park in the countryside, as it's a lovely day today.

'Which one are we going to, Clyde?' Connor asks.

'We will be heading to a place known as Hallows Walk. It is a picturesque location that is not often frequented by many people, with vast open fields, winding paths, and dense woods.' Clyde replies.

'Oh yeah, that sounds nice. Have they got somewhere there you can eat and that?' Connor asks.

'Yeah, of course they have. It is just such a lovely area,' Clyde answers back.

They arrived at a picturesque car park, surrounded by vibrant flowers in all shades of the rainbow. The edges of the car park were lined with blooming gardens, adding a touch of natural beauty to the scene. In the centre of the park stood a magnificent fountain, adorned with a cherub holding a basket that poured water into the pool below. The gentle trickle created a soothing melody that filled the air. It was a tranquil oasis.

Connor and Clyde both step out of the car, their feet crunching on the gravel driveway. They make their way to the entrance of the country park, a winding pathway lined with tall, ancient trees that cast dappled shadows in the afternoon sun. As they walk down the path, it feels like entering another world, closed off from the reality of life. The leaves rustle and whisper in the gentle breeze, and the air is filled with the sweet melodies of birdsong. Connor's ears pick up the soft chirping of robins and the melodic trills of finches. The scent of pine and earth fills his nostrils, reminding him of childhood hikes through the forest.

As they approached the end of the path, a vast field stretched out before them, adorned with delicate white and pink blossoms. Here and there, bursts of bright yellow flowers added a splash of colour to the serene landscape. They continued along the pathway that wound through the field, their feet brushing against soft blades of grass and wildflowers. The warm sun shone down upon their faces, filling them with a sense of tranquillity and contentment. The gentle breeze carried with it the subtle fragrance of flowers and the distant sound of buzzing bees. It was a perfect moment in time, one that they both wished would last forever.

Connor ponders whether he should broach the topic of Clyde's aunt and how he might be feeling. Knowing Clyde's aversion to discussing his emotions, Connor is hesitant to bring it up.

'How are you feeling now with the passing of your aunt?' Connor asks.

'I am feeling fine. It was sad at first, but we all knew it was coming for her. It was just a matter of time when it happened.' Clyde answered.

'Can I ask then if you knew it was coming how comes you never told me about it?' Connor asks.

'There is nothing to talk about. I do not need to tell you every detail about my family life.' Clyde's answers back

'But you don't tell me anything about your family life. I know nothing about them.' Connor says.

'You do not need to know about them. That is the part of my life that is separate from you,' Clyde says back.

'Isn't that a bit strange? I have never heard of that before, where your lover keeps his family separate. Do you not get on with them or something?' Connor asks.

'Yes, I do but really and truly I do not wish to talk about it.' Clyde replied.

'I just want to get to know your family. After all, you have met some of my friends. I mean, ok I know you haven't met my family. My mum, dad and sister live in Australia and that's pretty expensive to get to and from. I have only ever been able to afford it once,' Connor says.

'Can we drop it now as it is starting to really get on my nerves? I have nothing left to say. We can just go to my aunt's funeral and that will be it for family events from me for a while,' Clyde says.

'Ok. I just wished I could understand the whole of you, including your family and friends.' Connor says.

'I have no friends; I rarely see my family. That is all you need to know and all I need to know is you and that is all I want. You, just you, no one else.' Clyde answered.

The two of them continued to stroll through the peaceful countryside park, a comfortable silence settling between them. Connor's mind was racing, wondering why his family had to be hidden and why they could not discuss what had happened. Fear began to creep into his heart as he walked, feeling like he was floating along in a dream.

His thoughts consumed him, swirling with worries about the future and the consequences of falling in love with someone he may never truly know.

He is determined to find out more about this person. After all, they are now in a relationship, they have a house together and he cannot shake off the feeling of unease around them. Connor makes a mental note to gather as much information as possible, knowing it will help him understand the situation better.

After spending a few hours walking around the peaceful countryside park together, they both return to their car. As they drive away, Connor cannot help but wonder what the funeral will bring. He questions why he is even accompanying Clyde to his aunt's funeral if Clyde is so determined to keep him separate from his family. Despite feeling uncomfortable with the idea of interrogating his own relatives, Connor hopes that attending the funeral will provide some answers about Clyde. It seems like this may be his only opportunity to question his family about him.

The Morning of the Funeral.

Connor awakens and sits up in his bed, wearing Batman pyjamas adorned with the iconic yellow and black Batman symbol that he loves from the Tim Burton and Michael Keaton Batman movies. He gets out of bed and walks downstairs, noticing a familiar smell coming from the kitchen. Someone is cooking, and the delicious scent of bacon wafts through the hallway leading to the kitchen.

'Hey Connor, I have made us breakfast, Bacon and egg's as I know, you sometimes like a cooked breakfast in the mornings.' Clyde says with a big smile on his face.

'Aw, thank you Clyde, it smells really nice. Oh, look, you even done me a cup of tea, thank you,' Connor says back.

'No problem. You know I love to do anything to make you happy and smile.' Clyde says.

'Yes, I know you do.' Connor says with half a smile on his face.

'I have got your suit sorted out already. It is in the living room, hanging up. The service starts at 10:30am,' Clyde says.

'At 10:30am, oh ok, did you only just find that out then?' Connor asks.

'Well yes, I did. Why?' Clyde answered.

'I don't know. Usually, you find out days in advance what time a funeral is, especially a relative's funeral.' Connor answered back.

'Connor, please don't, not today. I cannot handle anymore pokes and prods into my family life and I am kind of questioning myself why you keep asking all this stuff like you do not trust me.' Clyde says.

'You're right, I'm sorry. I will stop and just be supportive of you today.' Connor says.

'Thank you so much.' Clyde says.

After finishing his breakfast with Clyde, Connor enters the spacious living area of his home. He glances at the grey silk suit hanging gracefully over the cabinet cupboard handle and makes his way towards it.

With a firm grasp, he carefully takes the suit off the hanger and heads into the bathroom to start preparing for the service.

Inside the warm steamy shower, Connor begins his morning routine by lathering his hair with rich shampoo. He massages it in before rinsing it out and repeating the process with conditioner. The scents of fresh herbs and citrus fill the air as he works through his hair, leaving it soft and manageable. Next, he reaches for his sponge and squeezes some shower gel onto it. Slowly lathering up suds, he gently cleanses his entire body. But suddenly, Connor hears shouting from outside the bathroom walls. The muffled voice grows louder and more urgent, causing him to pause and listen closely. It is difficult to make out what exactly is being said, but there is definitely someone in distress. Without hesitation, Connor turns off the water and steps out of the shower, ready to investigate.

Connor's heart races as he hears Clyde's voice shouting words so sharp and full of anger. 'Why is he shouting?' Connor scrambles to dry himself off, his heart pounding in his chest as he hears Clyde's command loud and clear:

'GO AWAY'. He rushes to get dressed, fumbling with his clothes as he tries to ignore the ominous tone in Clyde's voice. With a sense of unease, Connor exits the bathroom and enters the bedroom, only to find Clyde standing motionless at the window, gazing out with an unsettling stillness. As Connor approaches, he reaches out to touch Clyde's shoulder, but before his fingers can make contact, Clyde jerks away with a sudden and jarring movement that sends shivers down Connor's spine.

'WHAT, what.... what are you doing, Connor?' Clyde screams.

'I heard you screaming while I was in the shower. I thought something was terribly wrong. My socks and boxers are damp from the rushing to get dressed to see what was going on. You were shouting 'go away,' why were you shouting that? Who to?' Connor asks.

'There was a wasp in our bedroom I opened the window and tried to get it out. That is why I was shouting to go away.' Clyde answered.

'Oh right, ok then. I suppose if a wasp was coming out for me, I would shout worse things than that at the thing. They petrify me.' Connor says.

'Right, you need to get yourself all set to go. I am all ready, so whenever you are, we can just go to the service.' Clyde says.

'Yup, sure. I just need to do my hair and put my suit jacket on, then I am all set to go,' Connor says back.

Connor and Clyde head out, ready for their journey to pay their final respects to Clyde's aunt. The sun is shining brightly, its warmth providing a comfortable temperature despite the slight chill in the air. They reach the car and get inside, with Clyde taking the wheel. As they drive, they listen to the radio and hear updates on traffic conditions.

'Are you going to pick up any flowers to take with you?' Connor asks.

'No, I am ok. I will wait for the headstone and ground to be prepared before bringing flowers to decorate her grave.' Clyde replied.

'Ok yes, that sounds like a lovely thought.' Connor says.

As they arrive at their destination, Connor and Clyde park their car and step out into the quiet service. The attendance is minimal, with only a handful of people scattered around. They both stand outside, keeping their distance from the small group of mourners. The funeral car, adorned with flowers, sits near the entrance. Undertakers begin to remove the floral arrangements as they prepare to take the coffin away. Connor's gaze falls upon the relatives gathered, wondering which ones are Clyde's mother and father. All around them, the hushed sounds of grief and mourning fill the air, adding to the solemn atmosphere of the funeral service.

'Are you not going to go over and say hello to them?' Connor asks.

'No, it is ok. As I said, I am not that close with my family and we do not really talk much,' Clyde says back.

'Yeah, but you should really go and say hello. Today is a different day. You need to acknowledge each other on this sad day.' Connor says.

'No, I will be fine. Just attending the funeral service sitting at the back to pay my respects, then we will just go back home. All I want to do is get today over with, then go back to work tomorrow and get back to normal with things. Ok?' Clyde says.

'Yes, I understand.' Connor says.

As the pallbearers solemnly carry the polished wooden coffin on their shoulders, a hushed silence falls over the crowd gathered for the funeral service. One by one, they follow behind the casket as it is carried into the sombre chapel. Among them are Connor and Clyde, walking side by side with heads bowed. The melancholic melody of 'End of the World' by Skeeter Davis fills the room, adding to the heavy atmosphere. As they reach the back of the chapel, Connor cannot help but feel a sense of isolation and detachment from the service. The small number of attendees makes their seating at the back seem even further removed from the front, where the grieving family sits. It is an odd sensation to be so physically distant from such an emotional event.

The vicar proceeded with the service, his words carrying a weight of sadness in their melodic tone. He spoke of her life, of Angie Potts, a woman who had lived and loved with all her heart. Her life was filled with joy and love from her devoted husband and their daughter, sharing precious moments together that would be treasured forever. But then cancer came, uninvited and unwarranted, destroying their happiness and taking Angie away from them too soon. Through a long and difficult battle, Angie fought bravely but ultimately succumbed to the cruel grasp of the illness.

As the service came to an end, the vicar's final words lingered in the air like a soft prayer for Angie's soul. The coffin was slowly closed, enveloping her in a final embrace. And as if to symbolize the passing into another world, a red curtain was drawn around the coffin. Angie's family walked out of the chapel, each one carrying a piece of her spirit with them.

They gathered around the beautiful flowers that adorned her final resting place, brought by those who wanted to pay their respects and commemorate her life. And as they thanked the vicar for his moving tribute to Angie, they knew that she would always be remembered for the kind and loving person she was in life.

'Right, we need to go now.' Clyde says.

'GO? What, but we haven't even spoken to any of your family yet.' Connor says.

'Yes, I know, and I want it to stay that way. Seeing them the other night was way too much for me. They are horrible, selfish people.' Clyde says.

'Ok, well, do you mind if I go to the toilet before we go?' Connor asks.

'Yeah, just hurry though. I will wait in the car for you.' Clyde replied.

Clyde's footsteps recede as he walks towards the car, leaving Connor alone to fulfil his true intentions. Glancing over his shoulder to ensure he is unobserved; Connor sees that Clyde is completely out of sight. This is his opportunity to approach the grieving family members, pay his respects, and perhaps even discover their identity. With determined steps, Connor makes his way towards the group of people gathered for the funeral. His eyes scan the faces, searching for a sign of grief or sadness. Two individuals stand out among the sea of mourners, their faces etched with deep sorrow. These are the ones to whom Connor will offer his condolences.

With a sympathetic expression, Connor introduces himself to the grieving elderly couple. 'I am deeply sorry for your loss,' Connor says sincerely.

They both appeared to be in their late 70s, the woman with flowing blonde hair that cascaded down to her shoulders and a sharp dark grey suit that accentuated her elegant figure. The man stood tall with a full head of pure grey hair, combed neatly back, and dressed in a dark grey suit that matched his partner's attire. Their hands were intertwined, a sign of their enduring love and devotion to each other for decades. The lines on their faces told a story of a life well-lived and shared together.

'Thank you so much.' Said the woman.

'Yes, thank you. Can I ask how you knew Angie?' said the man.

'Yes, well, I don't know her. I am Clyde's partner, her nephew.' Connor replied.

The woman says back; 'she hasn't got any nephews, and I don't think she knows a Clyde neither. I don't wish to sound offensive but are you at the right service my sweet?'

Connor says back, 'My partner Clyde Hunter, he said this was his auntie's funeral.'

The man says back, 'we don't have anyone with the Hunter's name in our family.'

'Oh, I see. Excuse me, please.' Connor says.

Connor strides away, his steps heavy and determined as he feels the weight of the man and woman's confused stares piercing into his back. His heart races with adrenaline as he moves quickly towards the car where Clyde is waiting impatiently. With a sense of urgency, Connor reaches for the door handle, yanking it open and practically throwing himself into the car.

'Are you ready to go now?' Clyde asks.

'Yes, I am ready,' Connor says.

Connor's mind races with confusion, replaying the events that just unfolded. His chest tightens as he questions his own reality. Who is this person he shares a bed and a life with? And those strangers at the funeral, how do they fit into Clyde's life? Connor's heart pounds as he wonders what secrets lie beneath the surface of his seemingly perfect relationship.

The car ride home was silent, the tension between Clyde and Connor palpable. Connor's mind was in turmoil, trying to make sense of the mysterious box he found under the floorboard. His gut told him to confront Clyde about it, but a nagging fear held him back. As his thoughts spiralled, he couldn't shake the name he saw on the medication label, Victor Sharp. Why did that name sound so familiar? Connor knew he had to dig deeper into this unsettling discovery, no matter the consequences.

After arriving home, Connor and Clyde both agree to make dinner and turn in early for the night. Clyde has work tomorrow, so this gives Connor a chance to focus on researching the mysterious box he found and uncovering the truth about Clyde's identity. Connor has been avoiding the reality of the situation, desperately hoping that Clyde is not involved in any of it. He wants to believe that Clyde is just someone who has distanced himself from his family and is creating a new one with the people he meets in life.

The morning sun barely peeks through the drawn curtains as Clyde leaves for another day of work. Meanwhile, Connor throws himself out of bed and hastily gets dressed, eager to begin his research on Victor Sharp.

Fingers flying over the keyboard, Connor frantically types in the name 'Victor Sharp' into the search engine. The results are sparse, but he finally finds an article from seven years ago detailing the admission of a man named Victor Sharp to Southport Psychiatric Hospital. It was believed that he had suffered a mental breakdown after a tragic accident involving his husband. Images of blood-soaked walls and lifeless bodies flash through Connor's mind as he reads on.

According to the article, there were warning signs that Victor was planning a violent rampage. His target? The Black Harbour pier, where his husband had tragically lost his life in a rollercoaster malfunction. With horror, Connor imagines the chaos and destruction that could have occurred if Victor had carried out his plan. But it was not just the potential victims who suffered. Victor's husband had been flung from the broken rollercoaster and drowned in the sea below. A shiver runs down Connor's spine at the thought of such a gruesome death. Now more determined than ever, he continues his search for answers about this mysterious and possibly dangerous man named Victor Sharp.

As Connor's mind wanders, he cannot help but imagine the unimaginable pain of watching your beloved husband die in a gut-wrenching and traumatic way. The weight of such a tragic event could shatter even the strongest mind, leaving it consumed by impenetrable darkness. And to add on top of that, losing the love of your life - it's almost too much to bear. The thought alone sends a chill down Connor, reminding him of the fragility of life and how one moment can change everything.

Connor's head is throbbing, his thoughts scrambled and chaotic. He knows he needs to find the box again, to make sense of what is happening. He rushes up the stairs, his heart pounding as he flings open the bedroom door. With shaking hands, he pries open the floorboard and reaches for the box with a desperate need. But the lock is stubborn, taunting him with its tiny size. Connor grits his teeth in frustration as he fumbles with a paperclip. Connor's hands shake as he finally manages to pry open the sealed box. Anxiously, he surveys the contents and relief floods through him as he sees that all the items are there. His heart races as he reaches for the mobile phone and flips it open, hoping for some sign of life. But his stomach churns as he sees the blank screen, no messages or missed calls. In a sudden realization, he knows that Dr Starbuck was the one desperately trying to reach out on this very device before meeting his untimely end. The weight of the situation hits Connor like a ton of bricks, leaving him reeling with overwhelming grief and shock.

Was this box left behind by the previous owner, or does it have something to do with Clyde? Connor's thoughts race through his mind. 'Finding out about Dr. Starbuck cannot be a coincidence,' he thinks. 'I searched for him too and discovered that he died on the night of our halloween party.'

With trembling hands, Connor reaches into the small box and pulls out a plain envelope. As he opens it with shaking fingers, his heart races in anticipation. Inside is a photograph that steals Connor's breath away - an image of someone who could be his mirror image. Stunned, he stares at the striking resemblance between himself and the man in the photo, feeling a surge of shock and curiosity course through his veins.

Staring at the picture, Connor's heart races as he realizes the striking resemblance between himself and the person in the photo. The hair, eyes, and even the shape of their face and head are identical. In the background, the Black Harbour pier looms with its infamous rollercoaster, Need for Speed. Trembling, Connor flips over the photo to find eerie words scrawled on the back: 'I'll be with you again soon.' A chill runs down his spine as a sense of foreboding consumes him.

After snapping a photo, Connor carefully places everything back inside the box, locks it, and conceals it to make it look as if it has not been touched. With determination, he pulls out his phone and dials Rex's number.

'Hi Rex'. Connor says on the phone.

'Hey Connor, you, ok?' Rex says.

'Not really, I have just gone through that box again as everything is just playing on my mind. Clyde's funeral to his auntie was weird, and I found a picture in the box that I missed last time.' Connor replied.

'What was the picture?' Rex says back.

'It was the husband of this Victor Sharp, who died in an accident but Rex, it is the spitting image of me like right down to the shape of my head,' Connor says.

'Oh my god, are you serious? That's baffling. If you want to talk about it, I could come over. I am actually off work today, so I am free to come round.' Rex puts to Connor.

'Yeah, just come round when you can,' Connor says.

'Ok, I will be round shortly.' Rex replied.

'Ok then bye, see you soon,' Connor says back.

After ending the call, Connor makes his way down to the kitchen and fills up the kettle to make some tea. His mind is swirling with thoughts, and he leans against the counter, gazing out of the window. He cannot stop thinking about everything that's been happening, and he's starting to suspect that Clyde is involved somehow. It is the only explanation that makes sense but what if Clyde is actually Victor Sharp? And why do I resemble this person in the photo so closely?

A sudden knock jolted Connor, and he knew it was Rex. He quickly opened the door, and they both walked into the kitchen, where Connor repeated what he had found. He desperately wanted his best friend to give him a reasonable explanation for all of this and calm his nerves about the strange situation.

No matter what Rex says, Connor cannot shake his unease. It is becoming clearer that Clyde might be Victor Sharp and that he was the one who had a breakdown. He was admitted to the hospital and now has a new partner who looks exactly like his late husband.

Rex attempts to comfort Connor, but also subtly suggests that they ask Clyde about the mysterious box. As the situation becomes increasingly unsettling and confusing, it may be necessary to confront Clyde and address the issue. Keeping this information stored in one's mind is not a healthy way to live.

Connor and Rex come to the decision that the best course of action is to address the situation with Clyde directly and hear his explanation.

As the clock ticks closer towards 5:00pm, Rex heads home. Clyde usually arrives around 5:15pm. Connor mentally rehearses what he wants to say and how he can initiate the conversation with Clyde.

As the clock strikes 5:20pm, Clyde enters through the front door where Connor is already waiting for him.

'Hi Clyde'. Connor says.

Clyde greets me with a question, 'Did you wait for me by the front door?'

'I was actually. I found something upstairs and we really need to talk about it.' Connor says back.

'Ok, sure thing.' Clyde replied.

Connor and Clyde enter the kitchen and take seats at the table. Connor goes on to recount his discovery of the box under a floorboard in the bedroom, inside the wardrobe. He then elaborates on the link between the box and both Dr. Starbuck and Victor Sharp. Clyde wears a puzzled expression as he listens intently.

Clyde says to Connor, 'that is a very scary find, isn't it?'

'Is that all you got to say? Do you not know where I am going with this or what I am even trying to ask you?' Connor says.

'No, what are you trying to say?' Clyde replied.

'Are you Victor sharp?' Connor says.

Clyde's face twisted in confusion as he heard the name 'Victor' slip out of Connor's mouth. 'No, my name is Clyde, not Victor,' he corrected, shaking his head. 'I have no idea who this Dr. Starbuck is. Why are you asking me such a terrible question? Are you suggesting that I have been lying to you all this time?' He gestured at their shared home, as if it were proof of his honesty. 'If I was really this Victor Sharp, don't you think I would have left some evidence by now?'

'Yeah, but that is why I am asking you. It is all leading to you well in my head it is, anyway.' Connor says back.

'Oh my god, this is stupid. I have just come in from work and you are questioning me about whether I am who I say I am. What about this Dr's murder, do you think that was me too?' Clyde asks.

'Well, it's pretty suspicious that you come home that night of the halloween party with ripped clothing and splattered blood.' Connor says.

'I did that last minute, so I was not even more late to your party. if I were even later, you would be annoyed at me like you sometimes get,' Clyde says.

'I don't get annoyed at you,' Connor replies.

'Yes, you do. You are sometimes like a spoilt brat that if you do not get your own way, you sulk,' Clyde says.

'No, I do not. We are not talking about me. What about when you had a black eye?' Connor says.

'I told you I did that on the freezer door in the shop,' Clyde replies.

'No, you told me about the shelf in the shop, you walked into it.' Connor says back.

'Oh, for god's sake, door, shelf it's the same I don't remember all I know I was in the shop, and I got a black eye because I was not paying attention.' Clyde says to Connor.

'None of this makes sense. Why is there a box in the wardrobe?' says Connor.

'I do not know. You are not listening to me. I do not know about it, and I do not know why you are giving me all this grief. I Have done nothing but be kind to you and show you love; I have not had a relationship for a long time. I thought we were happy and finally living my life to the best I can but now I found out you are not happy.' Clyde says.

'I was happy until all this stuff came up. What about all the weird stuff going on with the letter? What about the knocks at the door?' Connor says.

'How am I supposed to know? What is the matter with you, and you are obviously not happy, otherwise why would you bring this to me thinking that I am someone I am not? I am literally just so upset by this whole thing,' Clyde says.

'You act shifty. You don't speak to your family and friends but act as if you have them, then act as if you have no friends and are not in contact with your family. I spoke to an older couple at your auntie's funeral, and they had not even heard of you.' Connor replied.

'I have done nothing wrong for you to treat me like this,' Clyde says.

'Everything seemed great and then all this weird stuff started happening. Then I found the box. We went to your auntie's funeral, where you stayed at the back and people hadn't even heard of you.' Connor says back.

'Well, I tell you what then why don't you get your stuff and get out? You obviously do not trust me and think I am the kind of person who lies about their identity, and you obviously think I am some kind of killer, too.' Clyde says.

'I didn't say you were a killer.' Connor replied.

'That Dr was stabbed forty three times. You are suggesting I am that person. How could you think I could do something like that?' Clyde asks.

'You lose your temper very easily.' Connor says.

'Oh, I see, so I must be some sort of crazed killer who had been admitted to hospital.' Clyde says.

'I did not tell you they admitted Victor Sharp to the hospital.' Connor says.

'That is enough. Get out, just get out. You can get your stuff another day.' Clyde replied.

'We need to talk about' Connor starts to say until Clyde shouts.

'GET OUT NOW.'

Connor rises from his seat at the table and heads towards the front door. He grasps the doorknob and turns it, pulling the door open. As he steps out, he looks back at Clyde, who is still seated at the table, staring at him with a menacing and dark expression. Connor is relieved to leave the house, feeling unsettled by Clyde's angry demeanour. As he walks down the street, Connor considers going to either Rex's or Susan's house, but decides on Rex's since it's closer. He turns the corner and continues walking for about ten minutes until he arrives at Rex's house. He knocks on the door and Rex answers.

'He threw me out. He got so angry that he threw me out.' Connor says.

'Gosh, come on, you are going to have to stay here.' Rex replied.

'Thank you. I just don't know what to do or say. He told me it is not even connected to him, and he felt hurt that I could even think that he is someone that he is not. He felt hurt that I thought he could kill someone in such a gruesome way.' Connor says to Rex.

'I do not know what to suggest. It is just very weird how all this evidence is suggesting that he is this Victor Sharp, yet there is no hard evidence to prove that it is. I mean, we could be wrong, or you may have just had a lucky escape.' Rex says.

'Just nothing makes sense at all. I mean, what about them two letters and someone scaring me in the night from two months ago?' Connor says.

'I think you should probably talk to him again tomorrow.' Rex answered.

'Yeah, maybe I'll just go back there tomorrow and just talk more about it.' Connor replied.

'Well, you can stay here as long as you like, as I have the spare room you can stay in, just until you sort this whole mess out.' Rex says.

'Thank you, you're a good friend,' Connor says back.

As the sun sets, Connor rises from his spot next to Rex and makes his way to the spare room. He arranges the pillows just how he likes them and slips into the cozy bed. His mind is running a mile a minute, replaying the events of the day over and over again. Clyde had convinced him to quit his job, promising that with his wealth they could live comfortably together. But now, lying alone in this unfamiliar space, Connor cannot help but doubt his decision. He has no home, no job, and possibly no relationship with Clyde anymore. Sitting up in bed, he agonizes over whether he was wrong about everything and if Clyde is truly innocent. Or was it all just manipulation? With a heavy heart, Connor eventually succumbs to sleep, hoping to gain some clarity and make a plan for tomorrow.

The clock reads 7:15am as Connor's eyelids flutter open. He rises from the bed and makes his way to the wardrobe in the spare room, where Rex has kindly left some clothes for him to wear. Luckily, they are the same size, and Connor did not bring any of his own. After selecting an outfit for the day, Connor heads to the bathroom for a quick shower. Once he is finished and dried off, he changes into the clothes and heads to the kitchen where Rex is waiting.

'Morning Connor, I heard you was up and made you a cup of tea,' Rex says.

'Morning, thank you Rex,' Connor replies.

'What you going to do?' Rex asks.

'I do not know; I might just go round and see if he is there.' Connor replied.

'Well, I hope it goes well and you get more information.' Rex replied.

'Yeah, me too,' Connor says.

Connor takes the final sip of his steaming cup of tea, savouring the warmth and comfort it provides. With a determined nod, he decides it's time to confront Clyde and try to make sense of everything that has been happening. Leaving Rex's house, he steps out onto the street, making his way towards his house. The familiar sights and sounds of the urban landscape surround him as he walks, his thoughts consumed with anticipation for their conversation.

He reaches the end of the street and catches sight of his house, a small but welcoming abode nestled among the other buildings. As he approaches, he notices the vibrant flowers blooming in his garden, adding a touch of colour to the surroundings. Finally reaching his front door, Connor fumbles for his keys and unlocks the heavy wooden door, pushing it open to reveal his humble yet comfortable home. Connor steps through the threshold of the door, surveying the familiar surroundings of his home.

His eyes immediately dart to where he knows the car keys are usually kept, but they are conspicuously absent. He moves into the kitchen, taking in the sight of a half-empty cup and a plate with crumbs scattered across it. It is clear that Clyde had breakfast before heading off to work. A twinge of uncertainty tugs at Connor's gut as he considers his options. Ultimately, he decides to pack a small bag with essentials and make his way back to Rex's house for the time being. Maybe he can reach out to Clyde from there and schedule another discussion about their current situation. The air feels heavy and fraught with emotion as Connor gathers his belongings and prepares to leave.

An hour has passed, and Clyde still has not returned, prompting Connor to make his way back to Rex's house. He decides against using his car since it is only a short distance to walk and there wouldn't be any parking available outside Rex's house. Connor grabs his bag and heads out the door, but not before leaving a note for Clyde on the cabinet by the entrance.

The note reads 'hi Clyde, I came round to talk to you, but you were not here. I will message you later to arrange a time to come back to have another discussion.'

Connor walks out of the door; he slowly walks down the quiet streets towards Rex's house. His steps quicken as he approaches the house, but his hand hesitates as he reaches for the door – it is already slightly ajar. Frowning, Connor pushes open the door and creeps inside, the darkness of the hallway engulfing him. Every fibre of his being screams at him to turn back, but he presses on towards the kitchen, his skin crawling with unease in the suffocating darkness.

As Connor makes his way down the hallway, he notices a sudden shift in the atmosphere. The once open curtains to the kitchen are now tightly closed, casting an ominous shadow over the corridor. A sense of unease creeps over Connor as he enters the darkened kitchen, struggling to make out any shapes or objects in the dim light. Connor enters the kitchen when suddenly, his foot slips on a slick substance and he falls hard onto the cold tile floor. Panic sets in and he frantically looks around for any sign of danger.

'Ouch, what the hell?' Connor speaks out loud.

Connor's body jolts upright, his elbow throbbing in pain from the fall. He staggers to his feet and stumbles towards the curtains, yanking them open in a panic. When he turns around, time seems to slow down as he takes in the horrific scene before him. A pool of crimson blood stains the floor, with clear slip marks leading towards it from where Connor had fallen. As he scans the room, his eyes lock onto the table where Rex sits slumped over, his arms splayed out in a grotesque display. Connor's heart races as he rushes to Rex's side, grappling with his lifeless body and screaming for him to wake up.

'REX…. REX…. Oh, my god please…… please no……oh god,' Connor cries out.

Connor carefully lays Rex's lifeless body back onto the table where he had found him, slumped over. He reaches into his pocket and retrieves his mobile phone, quickly dialling 999.

'Hello which emergency service do you need?' The 999-service line said.

'Ambulance please,' Connor replies.

'Hello, ambulance service'. The call handler says.

'Hi, my… my friend I just came to his house and found him in the kitchen, there's blood everywhere, his arm… it has been cut…. He's not moving.' Connor says.

'Ok, what's the address?' Call handler asks.

'129, Caps Road, Southport.' Connor replied.

'Ok, an ambulance has now been sent out to you they should be with you very shortly.' Call handler says.

Call handler also says, 'is your friend breathing?'

'I don't know, no, no he's not, he's cold. I was only here a couple of hours ago. He's cold.' Connor cries

'The body is cold?' the call handler asks.

'No, my friend, my friend is cold. What should I do?' Connor asks.

'Just wait for the ambulance they should be with you any second now.' Call handler says.

In the distance, Connor can hear the blaring of an ambulance siren. With a sense of urgency, he makes his way to the front door and opens it just as the ambulance pulls up. Two men quickly exit the vehicle, one carrying a medical bag. They approach the front door where Connor is waiting.

'Hi.' Paramedic says.

'Hi, he's this way, in the kitchen.' Connor says.

Connor's heart races as he follows the two men down to the kitchen, their hurried steps echoing in his ears.

They rush past him and immediately get to work on Rex, their hands moving with precision and urgency. Connor feels like a mere spectator, his body tingling with anxious energy as he watches them. His grip tightens on his mobile phone, his knuckles turning white from the pressure. The call handler's voice cuts through the chaos, with trembling fingers, Connor brings the phone to his ear.

'Thank you, they are here... I have to make a call.' Connor says.

Connor hangs up the phone on the call handler. Tears run down his face, his hands trembling uncontrollably as he looks up at the paramedic who approaches him with a sorrowful but sympathetic look on his face. 'I'm so sorry, I have to inform you, your friend has passed away,' he says, his voice heavy with regret. 'His heart must have stopped beating for over an hour now.' Connor looks over at Rex's body, his fingers have already started to turn a sickly shade of purple. As the gravity of the situation sinks in, Connor's whole body begins to shake with grief and despair. 'I am truly sorry for your loss,' the paramedic continues, 'we will need to call for a coroner to come and retrieve the body.' A wave of overwhelming sadness washes over Connor as he struggles to process the finality of his friend's passing.

With practiced efficiency, the paramedics carefully repack their equipment back into their bag. The faint smell of antiseptic lingers in the air as they make their way towards the door. Connor watches them intently, as they exit the house, Connor follows them down the winding pathway, their footsteps echoing on the pavement.

The bright lights of the ambulance illuminate the street. The paramedics open the doors and prepare to climb inside when Connor's voice breaks through the air.

'Thank you!' he calls out, his voice filled with gratitude and emotion. The paramedics turn and nod in acknowledgement before climbing into the ambulance and driving off, leaving Connor standing alone in the quiet. The image of the moving ambulance fades away as he watches them go, feeling grateful for their quick response and sympathetic care.

Connor makes his way back to the doorway and takes a seat on the doorstep, still clutching his phone tightly to his chest. He decides to give Clyde a call first, then he will reach out to Rex's parents who now reside in New Zealand after retiring there.

'Clyde, it's Connor. Please, if you receive this message, come to Rex's house immediately. Something terrible has happened...he's dead. I don't know what happened. Just please come.' Connor leaves a desperate voicemail for Clyde.

Sitting on the doorstep, Connor quickly dials Rex's mom, and she picks up after just one ring. He recounts the events that have unfolded and all he can hear in response is screaming and yelling. Her voice is shaky and it is clear she's barely holding it together. After only thirty seconds, the call abruptly ends. It must be unimaginable to receive news of your child's death like that.

Fifteen agonizing minutes have passed, the deafening screech of a car pulling up echoing through the empty streets. Connor remains motionless on the doorstep. Suddenly, he looks up and sees Clyde's car pulling in front of the house, tires squealing on the pavement. As Clyde jumps out and rushes towards him, Connor can barely contain the overwhelming surge of emotion building inside him. In one swift motion, Clyde wraps his arms around Connor, who lets out a gut-wrenching scream of despair. Time seems to stand still as they both struggle to get up from the doorstep, finally making their way into the house. The short hallway feels like an endless maze as Clyde leads Connor towards the kitchen. It is there that Clyde stops abruptly, gasping in shock and turning back to face Connor. A single word escapes his trembling lips: 'No...'

'I am so sorry. I am really sorry.' Clyde says.

'I don't know what happened. I was here two hours beforehand. Clyde, it looks like he's cut his wrist,' Connor says.

'It does, it really does.' Clyde says.

'Why...why...how I just don't get how,' Connor says.

'Do you want to go?' Clyde says to Connor.

'No, I can't. I have to wait for them to come pick him up. There is nobody that could get here to wait,' Connor says.

Connor leaves the house and Clyde trails behind him. Connor takes a seat on the front steps and buries his face in his hands. After a few moments, he raises his head to gaze at the darkening sky above.

'I'm going to have to clean. I can't leave that kitchen like that. He would absolutely hate it with it looking like it does.' Connor says.

'Of course, I will help you.' Clyde says.

'Are you sure? I wouldn't blame you if you left, especially after the fight we had.' Connor says.

'I am positive. We can talk about that at a later stage. Right now, is about you and helping you,' Clyde says.

'Thank you, Clyde. I am so happy you could come. I think I would have fallen to pieces if you hadn't come here.' Connor replied.

'I love you. We had a big fight, I know. We will sort that out. This is more important right now. Now let's go inside, do this horrific clean and wait for Rex to be picked up.' Clyde says.

Connor and Clyde worked together, gathering cleaning supplies from Rex's kitchen cupboards to tackle the gruesome scene on the table and floor. The metallic scent of blood hung heavy in the air as Connor gingerly picked up a sponge, its bright pink colour now stained with dark red. With careful movements, he soaked up the sticky liquid and squeezed it out into a nearby bucket. Meanwhile, Clyde sprayed down the table with an array of cleaning products, determined to remove every trace of the violent act that had taken place there. Their faces scrunched in concentration as they scrubbed and wiped, their efforts slowly turning the once-bloody surfaces back to their original state.

The task was almost complete, and Connor remained on his knees, his hands still slick with the blood. He could not tear his gaze away from Rex's lifeless body, feeling lost and numb as he stared at his best friend's pale face. The room seemed too quiet, too still, as if even the walls were mourning their loss. Connor tried to make sense of it all, but his mind was a blur of conflicted emotions. Grief, anger, guilt - they all swirled together in a storm that threatened to consume him. This was not how it was supposed to end, with Rex lying cold and motionless before him. But there was no changing it now, and Connor could only sit and mourn the loss of his dear friend.

Two hours passed and there was a loud knock that sounded at the door. Connor, who had been in the kitchen, walked down the hallway to answer it. He pulled open the door to reveal a man wearing white zip-up overalls that looked almost like plastic material. The hood of the suit hung behind the man's head, and his dark eyes scanned the room as he stood at the threshold. He was shorter than average, standing at about five foot five inches tall.

'Hello,' he said in a deep, serious voice. 'My name is Wes Raven. I received a call to come and examine a scene.' His tone was professional, but there was a hint of curiosity in his expression.

'Oh hey, yeah. My friend Rex he is in the kitchen. He had cut his wrist and died. Sorry, did you say examine?' Connor says to Wes.

'Yes, that is my job to come to a scene and just go over a few things before I have the body taken for an autopsy.' Wes Raven says.

'Oh, I am so sorry. We have cleaned up in the kitchen. I did not know this would happen.' Connor apologises to Wes Raven.

'Oh, you have? How much did you do? Only because I just need the scene exactly where your friend is.' Wes Raven says to Connor.

'I apologize, you should have been informed not to touch anything. Even though it may seem like a suicide, we are still required to conduct an examination and collect evidence for further investigation to confirm the cause of death,' Wes Raven replied.

'I didn't touch him, the way he is now is how I found him. There was a lot of blood covering the floor and there was so much blood that I am not sure I could have been here with the kitchen in that state.' Connor says.

'That is fine. As long as the body has not been touched, I should be able to carry out my duty. The ambulance crew should have really told you this,' Wes Raven says.

'To be fair on them, they had another emergency come in and they had to go, which I totally understand. Rex is just through the hallway in the kitchen. I will show you.' Connor says.

Wes follows closely behind Connor as they descend into the kitchen, where Connor gestures towards Rex's lifeless body.

'Thank you. It will not take me long at all. I have two colleagues outside waiting for the collection of your friend. You do not have to stay in here for this part while I examine him.' Wes Raven says to both Connor and Clyde.

'I will leave you to your business. I am going to go to his bedroom, just see if there is anything in there that would suggest why he did this. I just don't get it. He was happy, he was fine.' Connor says.

Clyde replies, 'he obviously was not happy. He must have been going through such terror in his head to even contemplate doing this, let alone actually doing it.'

'I just don't know. My head just feels so confused, it almost feels like I am floating. This does not feel real at all. I will go up by myself if that's ok. In case there are things that I need to conceal to keep his privacy.' Connor says to Clyde.

'Oh, of course, certainly. I will wait on the stairs until you are ready.' Clyde said back.

With heavy steps, Connor ascends the stairs that lead to Rex's room. He reaches the door and hesitates for a moment before turning the handle and pushing it open. The room is as clean and tidy as ever, each item in its designated place. Connor takes a few steps inside, scanning every corner of the room with his eyes. He opens the wardrobe, expecting to find at least some small sign, but it too is impeccably organized. As he continues to search the room, he realizes there is nothing here that could point to Rex taking his own life. The thought swirls in his mind:

why would Rex leave no trace? No note, no indication of his inner turmoil. Connor cannot bring himself to sit on the perfectly made bed, instead opting to stand at its edge and stare out onto the room, searching for any clues that may reveal the truth behind Rex's untimely death.

As Connor sinks down onto the crisp, neatly made bed, his heel brushes against something hidden under the edge of Rex's bed. Curiosity piqued, he lowers himself to one knee and peers' underneath Rex's bed. There, nestled in the shadows, is a small brown box that looks like it could be a shoebox. Connor pulls the box out and lifts off the lid. Inside, a collection of papers and cuttings lay scattered – articles from newspapers, faded photographs. As he sifts through them, he recognizes the article about the Black Harbour pier rollercoaster accident – the one that claimed the life of Victor Sharp's lover. And there, in another cutting, is the shocking news of Dr. Starbucks' death. Everything in this box seems to be connected to Victor Sharp – but why would Rex have all of this? The question swirls in Connor's mind as he stares at the contents before him, wondering what secrets may lie within this box.

With trembling hands, Connor rummaged through the box and his heart skipped a beat when he pulled out an old photo. It was the same one he had found tucked away in a box at his own house - the photo of the man who died on the rollercoaster ride. He turned it over, hoping to find some clue or message, but there was nothing on the back. Connor reached for another photo and pulled it out of the box. This time, it was a photo of himself and Clyde. A red heart had been drawn around Connor's face, while Clyde's eyes were viciously scratched out. Turning it over, Connor's blood ran cold at the words scrawled on the back: 'Soon I will be with you, Connor... Soon.' A chill crept up his spine as he tried to make sense of these strange connections and ominous messages.

The photo slips through Connor's fingers and falls to the ground. He stands up abruptly, feeling a jolt of shock course through his body. The air around him seems to freeze, as he tries to make sense of what he just saw. Everything feels still and silent, as if time has momentarily stopped in this moment of disbelief.

A sudden realisation hit Connor like a bolt of lightning - it was Rex all along. Every strange occurrence at his house, every piece of information that seemed to mysteriously appear, it was all because of Rex. Even the mysterious box that Connor stumbled upon in his home, could it have been planted there by Rex? The pieces were finally falling into place and a sense of unease settled in Connor's stomach as he realised the true extent of Rex's involvement in his life. His mind raced with questions and suspicions, wondering what other secrets Rex may be hiding from him.

'Clyde… Clyde, come up here.' Connor calls down the stairs.

With a burst of energy, Clyde sprints up the staircase and bursts into Rex's bedroom. His eyes immediately lock onto the box resting on the bed. Leaning over, he eagerly begins rummaging through its contents, taking care to examine each item carefully. Clyde straightens back up; his face was flushed and his hands clutching a few choice possessions from the box.

'Oh my god. It was him. Was he trying to break us up? This is exceedingly kind of scary stuff, what was going through his head.' Clyde says.

'It looks like he was maybe in love with me and hated our relationship and tried to get us away from each other. I just do not get it though. I have been friends with him for so many years, he gave no hints or clues to that he liked me in that way.' Connor says.

'It looks like it overtook him,' Clyde replies.

'Oh my god, you don't think he would have anything to do with Dr Starbuck, would you? No, he couldn't have. He was at our house at the party when that happened,' Connor says.

'Well, I suppose we do not exactly know what time that was,' Clyde says back.

'I… I cannot be here I just can't. I need to go,' Connor says.

'That is fine let's go. I will take you home,' Clyde replies.

Connor and Clyde both walk back down the stairs to be greeted by Wes Raven.

'Hi, just to let you know I am finished, and my colleagues have already taken your friend into the van. Someone should be in touch with you soon so you could make all the necessary arrangements.' Wes Raven says.

'Thank you, I have to leave myself now too.' Connor says to Wes.

'I am so sorry for your loss. You both take care now. Bye,' Wes Raven says to both Connor and Clyde.

'Take care too, Bye.' Connor replies

After leaving Rex's house, Connor and Clyde hop into Clyde's car and drive home. They enter their house and collapse onto the couch together, with Clyde holding Connor in his arms. They lay there in silence for about an hour. Eventually, Connor gets up and heads to the kitchen to make himself some tea. As he does so, Clyde joins him in the kitchen and starts talking.

'Are you ok? Sorry, I know stupid question; I just do not know what to say or do for you to make you feel better.' Clyde asks Connor.

'No, it's fine. I know you are just trying to be there for me. Thank You.' Connor says back.

'If there is anything I can do, then just tell me. I love you so much and would never want to lose you. The last day has been a nightmare for me. I thought all day that we were over.' Clyde says.

'I am sorry I questioned you about the whole situation. I just didn't know what to think or do.' Connor says.

'It is fine, look all that you had found and the weird stalking going on. You were bound to question everything. How were you to know that all this was actually Rex? I am just sorry that it all happened. I just want you to be happy and you should never be in pain like this,' Clyde says.

'I will heal in time. It will take some time to adjust to life without my best friend. Now, having all this knowledge that it was my best friend that has caused this, it may take a bit longer to heal,' Connor says.

'I will be here for you, no matter what. You are the best thing that has happened to me for like seven years. How about I get us a takeaway tonight?' Clyde suggests.

'I'm not sure I could eat anything; I mean, we can order that would be great but I'm sorry if I just can't eat it.' Connor says.

'It's fine, we will order and if you eat, it will be a bonus because at least I would be happy that you have eaten today.' Clyde says.

Clyde calls in for a Chinese takeout and orders a variety of dishes that he thinks Connor would enjoy. Meanwhile, Connor heads upstairs to take a shower and feels refreshed as he waits for dinner to arrive. After stepping out of the shower, Connor notices his reflection in the steamed-up mirror and wipes it away to reveal his face. He lets out a quiet sob and sinks to the floor, with only a black towel around his waist. He leans against the cabinet, crying silently but eventually struggling to contain his emotions. As his sobs become more audible, he covers his mouth with his hand to suppress the noise. Eventually, Connor composes himself and changes into his night clothes before heading downstairs to inform Clyde that the bathroom is now free.

'The bathroom is free.' Connor says to Clyde.

'Oh ok, thank you. I will go up and get a shower. Did that shower help you feel a bit better?' Clyde asks.

'Yes, it definitely did, thanks.' Connor replied.

'Ok then, food should be here soon, so I will be back in like ten minutes.' Clyde says.

'Ok sure, I'll get some plates out.' Connor replied.

Clyde climbs the stairs to use the bathroom. The sound of the bathroom door closing echoes through the house, and Connor takes this opportunity to go to the kitchen and prepare for their dinner. As he sets out plates and cutlery on the table, he sits down at the table with his expression remaining vacant. A knock at the front door interrupts his thoughts. He gets up from the table and walks over to open the door, revealing a tall man with long brown hair, black jeans, and a leather jacket, holding a bag of takeout food.

'Hi, thank you. That was quick. How much is it?' Connor says to the guy.

'Hi, it is £32.50 in total.' The takeaway guy said.

Connor checks his jacket pocket, which is hanging next to the front door, but cannot find his wallet. He turns to the man standing at the door, holding their food order with a scowl on his face.

'Sorry, one second I can't find my wallet.' Connor says to the takeaway guy.

Connor notices Clyde's coat lying on the ground and picks it up, searching through the pockets for his wallet. He finds a brown leather wallet in one of the pockets, containing some money. He plans to give this money to the delivery guy.

'Here you go, just take the £40.00. Thank you.' Connor says.

'Cheers buddy, enjoy.' Says the takeaway guy.

'Thank you, bye,' Connor says back.

As Connor closes the door, he takes the food with him to the kitchen. He sets it down on the counter and realizes he still has Clyde's wallet in his hand. Trying to get rid of it, Connor tosses it up in the air towards the table, but it falls short and lands on the floor. Bending down, Connor picks up the wallet to put it back in his jacket.

As Connor reached for the wallet, it suddenly flipped open, revealing a white square peeking out from one of its compartments. Curious, Connor carefully extracted the object and unfolded it, revealing a small photo. At first, he could not help but smile as he recognised himself and Clyde posing for a picture. But upon closer examination, his expression shifted as he realized that this was a photo of Clyde and the man who had died in the rollercoaster accident.

Connor's ears picked up the sound of the bathroom door opening and soon after, Clyde's footsteps coming down the stairs. As he entered the kitchen, Clyde saw Connor's expression - a mix of surprise and disbelief. Connor stood there, holding something in his hand that caught Clyde's attention.

'What is the matter, Connor?' Clyde asks.

'I've just found a photo in your wallet. It's of you and the guy who died on the rollercoaster accident seven years ago.' Connor says.

'You were not supposed to find that. I do it every time, once I did something, I always have at least one piece of evidence that could incriminate me. I suppose it is true what they say about people like me. There is always one thing that would link back to the story.' Clyde says.

'You… who the hell are you?' Connor cries out.

'Well, you have found out now. I literally cannot come back from you finding that photo. Yes, I am Victor Sharp and the guy in the photo was my husband. You obviously know he died, and I got very mad at that and tried to get back at the people who caused his death. I got found out yes, oh it took me a while to be rehabilitated, well me fake being rehabilitated, that is. I decided the only thing I could do was present to them how well I was doing. It took a few years to do so, as I was just not in a good place. I decided I was to find someone who looked exactly like my husband. That is when you came in.

When I saw you in that bar that night, I had to have you, so I pretended to bump into you while making it look like you bumped into me. I tried my hardest to win you over, which did not really take much, to be honest.' Victor said.

'You tricked me into your life because I look like your dead husband.' Connor said.

'My initial feeling was happiness. I got you to live with me. I persuaded to give up your job which by the way you had done so easily. That was easy. You and your friend, the friendship that you two had, was just so irritating. Do you know how many times I just wanted to kill Rex? I thought so many ways, so I started making you feel as though you had a stalker and also lucky for me. You ended up coming back here the day after our fight for me to kill him and make sure you found him. Oh god I had done so well until you found that bloody photo.' Victor says.

'So, you did kill Dr Starbuck that night and that was his blood on your clothes. You were going to let me think Rex loved me and stalked me and what you were going to be the hero that makes it all better.' Connor says.

'Well yeah, I was. What you have got to remember is that I mostly see my husband in you, so most of the time I look at you, I am not actually looking at you. I had to kill the Dr I mean, the calls did not stop, and I knew it would only be a matter of weeks before he notified the police that I was not checking in with him.' Victor said.

'You killed Rex and planted that box underneath his bed.' Connor says.

'Yes, I did, I loved slicing his wrists. You should have seen his face when he knew he was going to die. I told him you know, just as soon as he took his last breath, I told him that he had to die because he was just so irritating' Clyde confesses.

As Victor speaks to Connor, he slowly moves forward while Connor takes a few steps back. Eventually, Connor ends up near the kitchen counter and instinctively reaches behind him to hold on to it as if to steady himself from shock.

Victor continues to talk, 'I am stuck with what happens now. You know my mind is not sitting well with this. It is hurting me. I do not know what to do. I mean, we could carry on the way we are. We are fine, are we not? We can still be happy, yes?'

Before Connor even answers victor he reaches round into the sink and clutches onto a small knife and proceeds to say, 'In your dreams.' Connor aggressively says.

Victor's face contorts with pure, unbridled rage as he lunges towards Connor, his hands like vice grips around his neck. He squeezes and pushes, crushing Connor's windpipe in a desperate attempt to suffocate him. But Connor is not defenceless. With the knife tightly clenched in his hand, he thrusts it upwards into Victor's forearm, causing him to release his grip and howl in agony as he falls to his knees.

Victor screams, blood pouring from his wound 'Look at what you've done to me... I'm bleeding!' His words are filled with hatred and pain, fuelling his desire for revenge against Connor.

With a swift turn, Connor's hand darts to the frying pan hanging among the other pots and pans. With a fierce grunt, he thrusts his arm up in the air before bringing it down with full force onto Victor's head. The resounding whack echoes through the room as Victor crumples to the ground, his body limp and unconscious.

Connor straightens his posture, coughing as he tries to catch his breath. He stands there for a moment, one hand clutching his throat. It dawns on him that Victor is now unconscious, and this is his chance to escape before he wakes up. Without hesitation, Connor dashes towards the front door, grabbing his phone and car keys along the way. As he reaches for the door handle, his keys slip from his grasp, but he quickly scoops them up and opens the door. He rushes outside, not looking back. As Connor walked down the pathway, he glanced back and saw Victor's unconscious body still lying on the ground. He sprinted to his car, quickly unlocking it and jumping inside. After a brief look around the car, he starts the ignition and speeds away. The only thought in his mind was to go straight to the police station for help.

After a five-minute drive, Connor arrives at the Southport police station. He quickly exits his car and rushes into the building, heading straight for the front desk where an officer is already stationed.

'Please, you got to help.' Connor pleaded.

'What's the matter?' Police officer asks.

'My boyfriend, he…he just tried to kill me, he killed my best friend, and he killed that Dr Starbuck.' Connor says.

'WHAT?' the police officer says.

'Yes, I've knocked him unconscious at my house you need to arrest him please.' Connor begs.

'Ok, ok, hold on. What is your address?' Police officer asks.

'159 Carny Road.' Connor says.

'Anyone available to check out a house on Carny Road 159, I repeat 159 Carny Road. Domestic disturbance.' Police officer says while talking into his radio.

Another police officer answers, 'on route sir, will check out domestic disturbance at 159 Carny Road.'

'They need to go into the kitchen. He's on the floor in the kitchen. There's blood on the floor.' Connor says.

It has been three minutes since Connor's arrival, and he now rests in a chair at the reception desk of the police station. He takes a sip of water as the radio crackles to life, revealing the voice of the officer who had gone to the scene.

'Er sir, there's no one here, the door is open but nobody at home,' Radio says.

Connor jumps up out of his chair and walks over to the desk to where the police officer was communicating with the officer that was now at Connor's house.

'You sure? The person making the complaint said someone was unconscious in the kitchen and blood was on the floor.' Police officer asks.

'Sir, unless they came round and cleaned up the blood and left. There's no one here.' Radio says out loud.

Police officer turns to Connor and says, 'There was nobody there, no blood but the door was open.'

'Then he woke up and has gone somewhere. You need to find him he's a killer, and he's very unstable, he is not a well person at all.' Connor says.

'Yes, that's fine I will get the forms. We can go into that room, and you can tell me everything and we will help you.' Police officer says.

'Ok, that's fine, at least if I'm here I am safe.' Connor said back.

Connor sits nervously in the chair by the reception desk, waiting for the man to return. He cannot help but think about Rex and the guilt he feels for bringing Clyde/Victor into their lives, ultimately leading to Rex's death. Lost in his thoughts, Connor ponders all of the 'what if's.' Suddenly, the police officer re-enters the reception area, snapping Connor out of his deep contemplation.

'Hey sir, I'm so sorry I have been called away somewhere, but I have assigned another officer to you they should be with you within fifteen minutes. Please, are you able to continue to wait?' Says the police officer.

'Yes, of course. I'll just wait here. Not a problem.' Connor replied.

After thirty minutes, the other police officer still has not shown up to take down any information from Connor. He decides to wait, knowing that as long as he is in the police station, he will be safe from Victor's reach.

Connor's phone vibrates, and he pulls it out of his pocket to see he has a text message from Clyde's phone. Connor opens the message, and it reads.

(Clyde) hi you, it's Victor. I know you have been to the police; I saw them come to the house. Susan is with me. She says hello.

(Connor) Don't you dare hurt her.

(Victor) come to the Black Harbour Pier. We are both there. No police or she dies. You know I am not bluffing.

As Connor reads the message, he sinks down into his chair. His mind races with questions - could Victor be lying about having Susan with him? Should he call her to see if she is, okay? Just as he unlocks his phone, another text comes through, the message reads from Clyde's mobile. Connor clicks on it and sees a photo of Susan, looking visibly distressed with blood streaming down her nose and a cut on her head. The reality hits Connor like a punch in the gut - Victor is not bluffing, and Susan's life is in danger. With a sense of urgency, Connor knows there is only one thing left to do: go to the Black Harbour pier where they are both supposedly located.

Connor scans the police station, trying to spot the officer he spoke with earlier. He stands up from his chair and moves towards the door, taking his time. Upon reaching it, the automatic doors swing open and he steps out to exit the building. Connor makes his way to the car park and gets into his car, determined to reach Black Harbour pier. As he drives, he racks his brain for a strategy to end this once and for all. Would involving the police be the best option but that would put Susan in danger of falling victim to Victor? He knows that his only chance is confronting Victor at the pier and praying for a peaceful resolution without anyone else getting hurt.

Connor's car pulled up to the pier. He sat in the driver's seat, his mind racing with fear and uncertainty. The realisation had hit him like a ton of bricks - he was in way too deep and had no idea what to do next. The thought of Susan being in danger sent chills through his entire body. He could not bear the thought of her getting hurt because of him. Victor was capable of anything and had already proven that when he mercilessly stabbed Dr Starbuck forty three times.

It was clear that Victor was not mentally stable, and Connor shuddered at the thought of what he might do to Susan if given the chance. Connor ponders the possibility of reasoning with someone who has committed such a heinous act.

The heavy thud of Connor's car door closing echoes through the entrance to the Black Harbour pier, announcing his arrival. His eyes scanning the darkened surroundings for any signs of danger. Reaching the entrance, he notices that a few metal poles have been forcibly removed from the gate and left scattered on the ground. With a sense of unease, Connor picks up one of the poles as makeshift protection and begins to climb through the opening where they were once placed. The darkness envelops him like a thick cloak, only the sound of crashing waves beneath the pier breaking through the eerie silence. As he cautiously moves forward, making his way along the wooden planks, a faint glimmer catches his eye in the distance. It is the dim lights of the nearby rollercoaster, standing tall and proud against the night sky.

The vibrant red rollercoaster loomed before Connor, its two massive hoops reaching high into the sky. A bold sign emblazoned with the words 'Need for Speed' beckoned to thrill-seekers at the entrance to the ride. Suddenly, a buzzing sensation in his pocket interrupted his thoughts. Connor reached for his phone and saw it was a text message from Victor, sent through Clyde's device as always.

(Clyde) I thought it would be fitting for you to come and get Susan from the Haunted House right next to the rollercoaster. You love horror, right? So let the horror continue. We are both waiting for you inside. See you soon.

Connor's eyes are drawn to the looming haunted house ride, standing next to the tall rollercoaster. Connor could make out two levels of the ghost train, with a carriage that would take brave souls on a hair-raising journey through both stories. The wooden exterior was weathered and painted in an eerie shade of brown, with faux windows displaying images of witches and devils inside. A ghastly Skellington figure stood at the entrance, its bony hand beckoning visitors to enter if they dared.

As Connor approached the entrance of the haunted house, he noticed a small door off to the side that seemed to be for staff only. Curiosity getting the better of him, he tried the handle and found it unlocked. With a slight creak, the door swung open to reveal a narrow corridor, lined with red lights and painted black walls.

As Connor steps down the dimly lit corridor of red lights, the sounds of the amusement ride surround him. The mingling with the mechanical hum of the speakers and the clanking of the carriages on their tracks. Suddenly, a devilish voice crackles through the speaker system, sounding like an old vinyl record playing on a scratchy turntable. 'Death is here,' it hisses, it's sinister tone sending shivers through Connor. 'You cannot hide, you cannot run... just give in to death.' The voice erupts into a menacing laugh, echoing throughout the corridor and adding to the unsettling atmosphere.

Connor makes his way down the dimly lit hallway, his footsteps echoing against the tiled floor. As he turns a sharp corner, he is met with the control room. However, his eyes are immediately drawn to a figure in the centre of the room. Shock courses through his body as he recognizes Susan, bound to a chair with silver tape wrapped tightly around her hands and feet. Her mouth is also covered in the same silver tape, rendering her unable to speak. Without hesitation, Connor rushes towards her, placing the metal pole on the floor next to Susan, his heart pounding in his chest as he frantically tries to wake her from her unconscious state.

'Susan...... Susan, please wake up.' Connor cries out.

As Connor's grip tightens on Susan's shoulders, her body begins to stir and awaken. With a determined pull, Connor peels the silver tape off of Susan's mouth, causing her to take in a deep breath that sounds almost like a gasp for air. The tape had been binding her mouth shut, making it difficult for her to breathe freely.

'Oh, my god Connor…… What the hell is going on, why is he doing this?' Susan asks.

'His name is Victor Sharp. He killed Rex and a Dr that used to treat him in the psychiatric hospital. He's not well and very unstable, he was only with me because I look like his dead husband from seven years ago.' Connor explains.

'Oh my god, that doesn't even sound real, he said nothing to me. I was at home, and he was just there in my living room when he attacked me. I didn't know what to do, I froze and then he hits me over the head with a vase and I woke up here with you.' Susan says.

'I don't actually know what he wants. I went to the police, but he messaged to come alone, or he would kill you,' Connor says.

'My Eva is asleep in her bed. She doesn't even know I'm here. There is no one at my house looking after her. She is all alone right now,' Susan cries out.

Connor unravels the silver tape from Susan's feet and arms from the chair.

'You're alone? You did not bring the police? Why?' Susan asks.

Emerging from the shadows in the corner, Victor appears

'Oh, don't be hard on him, Susan. He knows that if he were not alone that I would kill you without hesitation. It is not his fault.' Victor says.

Connor rises to his feet and turns to find himself face to face with Victor, who is gazing at both Connor and Susan. The blank expression on Victor's face gives away no emotion as he casually rests one hand on his hip and leans slightly to the left.

'So now what? What is going to be your plan now? Surely you do not think this is going to end good, do you?' Connor asks Victor.

Victor replies, 'well it is certainly not going to end good for you. Why would you think I would bring you here? I knew I would not get away once you had gone to the police. This would be my only chance to get you on your own.'

Connor replies, 'I really loved you; I can't believe Clyde does not exist and underneath that false character is someone so evil and unwell. I suppose your auntie isn't dead, and you were lying about that?'

'Of course, I was lying. You made it so hard. I actually thought this entire process was going to be really easy, but when you started to question me about where I had been or questioned me about my life. It started to get really hard for me to control myself, to just not end you and then possibly try again with someone else,' Victor said.

'But why? Why go through all that trouble? You had the chance to get better and have a life and be happy. I could have made you happy, but you chose this instead.' Connor says.

'I was happy. My husband made me happy until he was taken away from me. From the world... and nothing was ever going to be the same again.' Victor says.

'Why, why target innocent people? We were not involved in the accident of your husband. You killed two people, Victor, just to be with someone who looks like your husband,' Connor says.

'You do not just look like him, you could be him. Everything about you is just him. Apart from the constant questioning that is. He questioned nothing.' Victor said back.

'I just feel sad it had to end like this. I thought we were good together. I thought you were going to be my forever person.' Connor says.

'We still can be. I still love you. You stabbed me in my arm and hit me over the head with a frying pan, but I have done things to you so now I suppose we are even. I am still madly in love with you. I see my husband, yes, but I can make you happy. I can give you everything and be devoted to you, just like I was with my husband.' Victor says.

As Victor's expression mirrored his own sadness, Connor could not help the thought of grabbing Susan and making a run for it through the corridor. He knew the door was already unlocked and open, waiting for them to escape.

Connor grabs Susan and shouts, 'COME ON'

With their hearts racing and adrenaline pumping, Connor and Susan sprint down the corridor towards the door. But as they reach it, they slam into its solid surface, jolting them to a stop. Panic sets in as they frantically pull and push on the locked door, realising their escape has been thwarted.

Panic sets in as Connor scans his surroundings, searching for anything that could help them escape. He remembered the metal pole he had when entering the pier, now lays discarded on the ground next to the chair where Susan had been tied up. But there's no time to retrieve it as Victor comes charging down the corridor towards them. In the dim light, he can make out something glinting in his hand - a knife. Their chances of survival decrease with each step he takes closer.

Connor and Susan frantically scramble up the steep stairs that lay alongside the rail tracks of the

haunted house, they reach a dead end at the top, panting and sweating, realising there is nowhere left to run. Suddenly, Victor appears behind them with a glint of madness in his eyes and a gleaming knife in hand. With a gut-wrenching scream, he lunges towards Connor who barely manages to grab hold of Victor's wrist, fighting for control over the deadly blade. Every muscle in Connor's body strains as he tries to push away the knife that inches closer towards his chest. In desperation, he kicks out at Victor, causing him to stumble back and drop the weapon. Without hesitation, Connor snatches up the knife before Victor can even react, ready to defend himself at any cost.

Connor holds the knife in front of him, waving it back and forth in front of Victor.

Connor replies, 'We can be the same as we were, me and you. We can just leave and go and never come back. Just me and you and forget about what has happened here. I could be your husband and make you happy, just like he did.'

Victor replies, 'well, you did make me happy, and I would have done anything for you.'

Connor offers, 'We're here to support you and guide you towards improvement. You still have time to recover from this.'

'What in prison? I do not think so,' Victor says.

Susan walks alongside Connor, catching on to his plan to distract Victor and save their own lives. She also attempts to reason with Victor in the hopes of finding a peaceful solution.

Susan speaks, 'Connor has a point. We're here to help you. All you have to do is release us, and we can find you the help you need to get better. It may involve going to prison, but isn't your life worth saving? Why waste it?'

Connor's hand trembles as he grips the knife, knuckles turning white from the strain. He holds it out like a weapon, pointed directly at Victor's chest. Their eyes lock in a fierce stare, and with a swift motion, Connor swings the knife towards Susan's vulnerable neck. Blood gushes forth as the sharp blade slices through her throat, grasping at her own neck in a futile attempt to stop the bleeding. Crimson red splatters all over Connor's face and clothes, but he does not flinch. Instead, he turns to face Victor with a chilling expression of malice.

'Why?' Susan says as she starts choking on her own blood and could barely breathe.

'Why not? At least this way I will be loved and cared for. When am I going to find that again?' Connor says.

Susan stands against the railing of the walkway, blood gushing from her throat. With a forceful shove, Connor propels Susan over the side of the railings, and she plummets to her death on the ground below.

Connor and Victor both look down at her body from the second floor and see her take her last breath all the while she was staring at them both from below. A blood puddle starts to build up around her lifeless body as the blood was still flowing out from her throat. Connor and Victor both leaned back from staring down at her body to looking at each other.

Victor says, 'For a second, I actually thought you were trying to trick me just so you can get away.'

Connor replies, 'at first, I was. I mean I am not sure if that plan would work or not. I just thought in my head how much I was happy with you. You made me

so happy, and I just wanted that back. There is nothing here for me. We can be happy together.'

Victor says 'I would very much like that. We do not need anybody else but me and you. Now that I know you would be true to me, I could make a life somewhere with you.'

Connor replies, 'Killing Susan, I actually really liked that. The rush and adrenaline that came from that just felt so freaking good.'

Connor runs his hand over his face, smearing the blood that splattered on his face that now covers him. He clenches his fist and shuts his eyes, as if savouring the rush, he got from taking another person's life and absorbing it into his own.

Victor says, 'we should start going. You know we would be no good to each other if we get caught by the police or someone comes in here and finds her body.'

Connor replies, 'you're right, let's get out of here.'

Connor and Victor descend the stairs together, with Victor forcefully opening the locked door to exit the haunted house ride. They walk side by side, and as

they reach their destination, Victor slowly reaches out his hand to grab Connor's. Their hands intertwine tightly as they stand there, gazing into each other's eyes for a few moments. With huge smiles on their faces, they both turn their heads towards the looming Need for Speed rollercoaster. After admiring it for a moment, they turn and begin walking down the pier towards the entrance.

After crawling through the gate where the metal poles had been removed, Connor and Victor make their way to Connor's car. Connor unlocks it and they both get in, with Victor taking the driver's seat and Connor in the front passenger seat. They turn to face each other and after a brief five-second pause, lean in for a quick kiss. As they break apart, blood from Connor's face stains Victor's lips and face. They settle back into their seats and Victor starts the engine before driving away. With a wide grin, Connor watches as Victor licks the blood off his lips while they drive off.

The End.

Printed in Great Britain
by Amazon

44932795R00119